Tower in the Crooked Wood
By Paula Johanson

Tower in the Crooked Wood

Paula Johanson

Published by Doublejoy Books, 2020.

TOWER IN THE CROOKED WOOD

First edition. November 30, 2020.

Copyright © 2020 Paula Johanson.

ISBN: 978-1989966105

Written by Paula Johanson.

For Bernie and the twins, who gave me magic.

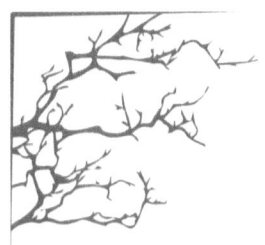

Chapter One

There. If that wasn't the cursed mountain she'd left bloody footprints on, Jenia didn't know where else under the two moons it could possibly be.

It looked familiar, at least: the cone shape slumped so the top third jutted to one side, making a shoulder. And maybe if this light rain ever let up completely, she'd see other familiar signs: the dead-white trees twisted in spirals, or the small, contorted pines, or the one truly frightening hemlock which rose out of a bog like a giant's pitchfork of bone. She would know them if she ever saw them again. Her luck was turning at last — Jenia hadn't seen the soldiers following her since she crossed the strait and came to this island. And since she awoke, there had been no sound or sign of wild beasts uncomfortably near.

Stepping out from under the canopy of tall trees, Jenia pushed her way through the thick brush and rough sawgrass along the shoreline. A flying insect whined at her ear, and she brushed it away. Around her the sounds changed from hushed quiet under the trees, where only a raven's call broke the soughing of wind in the branches; now Jenia felt the open space around her, where an osprey wheeled, screaming, and gulls fought over a dead fish. Waves pounded along the length of the beach, in a bay that curved between two points of land, one low and one higher. The calm, deep water was grey, reflecting the leaden clouds that closed in, giving off mist and a warm rain.

Jenia's oiled leather cloak and boots were still keeping out most of the rain, but under them her brown woollen shirt and trousers were damp. Pushing back her hood, Jenia ran her fingers through her sandy hair, cropped short for her brother's funeral, and stretched to relieve aches in places she hadn't expected to hurt until she was an old woman.

Nineteen summers is too young to ache after hiking and sleeping on rough ground, even though I've only been at it three months, she told herself, and pulled her hood forward again, keeping most of the light rain off her face. At this point she didn't care whether it was sweat or rain soaking her clothes. The sun

1

was getting low over the Western Sea, and if she didn't find a place to shelter soon, she was in for another uncomfortable night. Another whining insect landed on her hand and bit. She flicked it away.

More than the damp and the coming night's chill, Jenia worried about last night's unseen beast that had crashed through the prickle bushes only a few yards from her. She had huddled, barely breathing, in the dry nest she made for herself under a fallen log. Several times during the day she had wondered whether this beast was the one that had howled somewhere nearby as she was falling asleep, or the one whose wild cat-like scream had awakened her, hours later. Neither cry was any nearer than the next hilltop, Jenia was sure, but she had fallen asleep with her good bronze knife ready in her hand. It had been an unnerving night.

At least this coming evening wouldn't be a hungry one, she realized. The bushes along the shoreline were loaded with berries, deep purple dusted with blue, among the shiny oval leaves big as the palm of her hand. A small bird, speckled brown, darted among the branches and fled with a berry held in its beak. "Thank you, little one. No thorns," she said aloud. "What did I do to deserve this good luck? Though it is too early in the year for bramble berries. I wonder what these are called?" Jenia pulled a wooden bowl from her pack and picked the unfamiliar berries until it was full, keeping one eye on the sun as it dipped below the drizzling cloud cover. The berries the birds ate were usually suitable food for humans as well, and purple ones were always good here on the coast. She'd learned that from the friendly traders who brought her to this island with their boat. So that would be dinner, supplemented with a few bites of smoked fish from her pack. Now where could she get out of the rain? Maybe there was a thicket nearby, or she'd have to hole up under a fallen tree again.

A rustling almost underfoot made her leap backwards, one hand on the bronze knife at her hip. Out from the bushes and through the green-grey sawgrass pushed a small white dog, head down and watching her. It growled softly, as if it were unsure who she was or whether to trust her. "Good dog," Jenia said automatically. "Good boy. Where did you come from?" She offered her hand to the dog.

It didn't want to approach her yet, and knowing something of dogs, Jenia didn't blame it. She probably smelled differently from anyone it had ever known. "Good dog. Who gave you a good combing? You look neat and clean, way out here on the edge of nowhere." Taking a packet of smoked fish from her pocket, Jenia threw it a morsel, which was sniffed and then accepted in one swallow.

"Well, that's one more good sign," she said as she wrapped up the rest of the packet in its linen cloth and put it away. "Where did you come from, you greedy rascal?" She took up the bowl full of berries in one hand again, and turned to look along the curve of the grey beach, the brush and the tall trees growing close and dense as a field of grain, searching for some sign of people living here.

A voice calling from the bay behind her almost startled Jenia into dropping her bowl. People were coming ashore in narrow, open boats that looked as if they had been carved from tall trees. The dog pounded past her, barking happily, running down the beach to meet the strangers as they came out of their boats. Jenia waited where she stood, unsure of what to do with her hands, and wished suddenly her boots did not look so badly scuffed with travelling on hard roads and cross-country.

It was not long before someone came up the beach to meet her. "Instead of waiting to meet you as you come to us, we have to come ashore to meet with you," said one of the bare-chested men, his dark hair shot with grey. He carried a hat plaited of reeds or roots in one hand. "I am Talas, and our village is called Tlakwa. You are a stranger here," he added, looking over her travelling clothes of wool and leather. "Very strange. Are you welcome here? Where is your boat?"

"I'd like to be welcome here. I have no boat." She added, "I came across from the mainland to Copper Island in a trader's boat at Musky Creek." The dog ran back to her, panting, with damp sand flying from its small feet. It skidded to a stop and sniffed curiously at her hands and boots.

"Then you didn't come round the shore by boat? You walked through the highlands in the mountains?" Talas called the dog to him with a short whistle and a quick gesture, and it came to lean against his calf-length leather pants, then sit at his feet.

"Yes, through a river valley, over a ridge and down another river valley," Jenia told him, glancing past to the other people pulling their boats high above the tide line. "I had no idea Copper Island had such high mountains. It was a very hard journey. How do you get through them? I'm sure you have a better pass than the one I found."

"We don't," he said, and the friendly tone that had seemed natural to him was gone suddenly. "We don't travel there. It's forbidden. Poison ground. Strange beasts live there that can follow you and kill you if you're not lucky. We don't go there," he said again. "You ought to travel in a boat, like a decent person." The offshore wind that blew his hair into a wild halo around his head was suddenly cooler, as if in response to his words.

"I didn't know." Rainwater dripped off her hood into the bowl of berries. "I'm sorry I offended you." The dog's ears came up, and it ran to meet someone coming from the boats, which were all now pulled high on the beach.

"Is she welcome, Talas?" asked the approaching young person, putting out a hand to stop the dog from jumping up, then rumpling the soft, neat fur. It wriggled, and turned round for more petting. Plainly they were well acquainted.

"I don't know yet, Tsusiat. We'll have to find out." The rain was almost gone, only a faint mist falling in the late afternoon light. "We'll go indoors and ask questions around the hearth. I don't think we'll need to go to the questioning place."

Jenia was surprised to see from this position on the beach there were four large, wooden houses farther along the curve of the bay. If she'd climbed the headland or walked along the shore as they were doing now, she'd have seen the village and worried less about finding a dry thicket to shelter in for the night. The low point of land receded behind them. The near headland, an arm enclosing the bay, had a bare space above the cliff. There'd be a good view of the whole shoreline from so high above the water, but also a nasty drop to the water pounding on rocks below.

Now the smell of wood smoke was coming to her, and children's voices. "Come to my home," Talas said, calling her attention back to the people on the beach, waiting expectantly. "I hope to be able to call you guest and friend, when you have named yourself to us. Tell us the story of your travels, how you came here."

"I am Jenia don Dela don Tared," she said easily, but that didn't seem to be all he wanted to hear. They moved together towards the wooden houses which were constructed with great beams and posts high enough to catch the last amber sunlight that had already left the shore. "You already know how I came across Copper Island, and came here in a trader's boat." It was frustrating to walk on the loose grey sand slipping under her boots. "The roads and rivers I came by on the mainland wouldn't be familiar to you — I was told your people trade up and down the coast in boats, not inland where I came from."

While the rest of the people had left their boats and reached the houses already, Jenia walked along slowly, feeling she was losing half a stride with each step in the loose grey sand until she copied Tsusiat's way of walking along the logs washed up high on the beach by winter storms. These logs weathered silver by sun and rain were from the tall trees she had been walking under, Jenia could tell by the smell and grain of the wood.

Cedar, the traders called those trees, she remembered, *before I left their boat on the other side of Copper Island and walked over the island's backbone ridge under those trees.* The smells were so much stronger here — the cedar, pine and hemlock resins mixing with the salty air. She was learning about cedar now, as seasoned logs thudding under her feet, as well as trees standing tall on hillsides or rotting on the ground under the canopy of branches. Now she had seen it as seasoned wood long exposed to sun and rain, it was familiar to her in the same way as the peak she had glimpsed before the clouds closed over the low mountains, drizzling rain. She knew this wood was part of the reason for her journey.

The white dog trotted beside them along a great weathered log, keeping pace with the man's longer stride. "You should tell us how you came here so we know who you are," Talas said patiently. "Are you a hero or a spy? Are you a trader or a thief?"

She was shocked he could take her for any of those things. "I'm a, a, an arborist!" she stammered in protest. "A tree-shaper." Stumbling from the end of one log to another that rocked underfoot, she struggled to regain her balance. "I'm not used to travelling or adventures or any of that. You think I'm interested in spying on rain and gorse bushes?"

Talas watched her closely. "Is it a vision you follow or revenge? Is there a family lonely for you at your own hearth, or are you outcast? Unless you tell your story properly, we cannot know who you are." His bare feet moved confidently along the logs and between them on the loose sand, without him seeming to look where he walked. Jenia guessed his callused feet must be tough enough he did not worry about splinters or the odd stone in the sand. Tsusiat's sandals tapped along the logs, lightly as Jenia's scuffed boots.

They paused near the largest of the wooden houses, which stood as long from front to back as the great forest grew tall on the hillsides. "Unless we know who you are, we do not know how to receive you," said Tsusiat, standing quietly beside Talas with the dog underfoot like a white shadow. "How shall I put your name in a song?"

The idea of becoming part of a song was strangely appealing to her. *What would Tsusiat find to tell about me in a song? Would it be a melody, or a chant? What would anyone sing about plain little me, the youngest and smallest of my family — my very small family.* She shook the thoughts out of her mind, and brushed away another insect whining around her face. "I'm not here looking for you, anyway, I'm —"

"It will soon be dark and raining hard again. Come to our fire and evening meal." He bent to rub the dog's ears, scattering mist drops and the pungent smell of wet dog. "Tell us of your journey so we know whether you are our honoured guest or an enemy. If we don't like your story, Lema needs another slave woman to prepare hides." Talas smiled cheerfully.

Talas straightened and walked forward up the steep slope from the beach, and put one hand on the great wooden doors of the largest of the four houses. Faces and abstract designs were carved into the doors, and the marks of chisels were softened by the touch of many hands. Clearly this house had stood here for more than a handful of years, the doors swinging open to let in light as well as friends and family. "If we think you're lying," he added as the carved doors swung open under his broad hand, "we'll take you back up onto the headland and throw you off the cliff." The white dog slipped indoors, out of sight.

Jenia stared after him, startled. He had seemed so friendly — and as natural as the forest and sea around him. *Why would he make such a threat?* She had not learned, even yet, to be less than trusting among strangers.

"After all, you came over the poisoned land," Tsusiat said reasonably, as the dog peered around the door jamb. "You might be one of those beasts."

"I'm no beast!" The dog disappeared again into the house like a child's puppet.

"You know that, I know that. But Talas wants to learn it for himself," Tsusiat said, brown eyes sparkling with humour. "I've tried to tell him beasts from the poisoned land have fangs and many legs. Or stingers. But he still has his suspicions."

"Won't he be angry you're teasing him in front of a stranger?" It seemed likely. Jenia had already learned during her travels some people who spoke for their villages did not take criticism well.

"I'm not worried," said Tsusiat as frankly as if they were siblings. "Whenever he tries to tell me what to say or not to say, I put his name in a song that the whole village sings for a week." Tsusiat moved to open the door wider. Cooking smells drifted invitingly over a thread of wood smoke. Jenia's stomach rumbled with hunger, and she found herself wondering if what was cooking would taste as good as it smelled. It would be different from the turnips and cabbages at home, and there was fish cooking instead of red meat.

"So come and tell us your story. I promise you, Talas has thrown no one off the cliff who did not lie and cheat at games and steal and beat the slaves." Tsusiat's smile flickered. "And only one spy was ever sent back to the other traders naked in an open boat. We really do enjoy meeting new people, to tell stories like in winter when no one wants to go outdoors. Now it is time to go indoors." And Jenia let herself be brought inside the wide wooden doors, into the shadowy interior of the great wooden house with the rain drumming lightly on its roof of cedar planks.

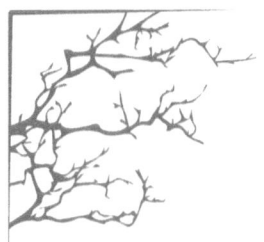

Chapter Two

The air inside was a little smoky. Almost immediately she noticed with relief there were no more of the small, flying insects that had plagued her. For Jenia, this house would be a blessing if for that reason only, and no other. There was no obvious reason the biting flies stayed outside the door; she wondered how it was done. *Nothing I tried myself during the night would keep the pests away.* She saw drying racks hanging under the high roof of planks, and gaps where smoke worked its way out without letting rain fall inside.

There were carved pegs set along a wall inside the door, where wet shawls were hung and cloaks spread out to dry. Several curiously woven hats were hung there as well. It was dark and smoky inside, and Jenia paused near the door to let her eyes adjust. She was shown a peg where she could hang her oiled leather cloak and small pack, while Tsusiat called a child to come take the bowl of berries.

Jenia gave up the bowl to be shared in the evening meal, and shook out her cropped hair, trying to finger-comb it into some kind of order instead of its usual tousled mess. "Who are these berries for?" lisped the child, shy in front of a stranger, and Tsusiat patted the small, round head for reassurance.

"Where did you gather these?" asked Tsusiat. With a start, Jenia realized it was she who was being addressed, not the child, as Tsusiat went on, "Where you were standing when we met you?" Jenia nodded. With eyes closed, Tsusiat sang a brief chant, in a low, true voice but almost inaudibly, in a sing-song way that reminded Jenia of the counting rhymes she learned as a child. "That is where your aunt Clata gathers, where the old houses were built in grandmother days," Tsusiat told the waiting child with the bowl clutched in grubby hands. "Tell her, Lop, so she won't think you got greedy."

It was good to be among people again, after so many days alone during the past months. Several times during the night, Jenia had heard sounds under the trees, rustling sounds of branches bending and bushes being pushed aside.

It had probably been nothing larger than a quick-footed raccoon, but her imagination had run away with itself, peopling the woods with bears and giant cats like the ones whose skins lay draped over the wooden benches which she was now able to see clearly, in the half-dark inside the Tlakwa house.

Oh, I'm glad I didn't see those furs before sleeping outdoors under a fallen tree, she thought ruefully. *There would have been brown cats, soft as smoke, instead of whiskery bob-tails in my dreams. I wouldn't have slept a wink, knowing the bears get this big here!*

Jenia wished she could relax. It was clear these people were not like the soldiers who had tracked her as far as the traders' boats on the mainland shore, but still she worried about the ultimatum Talas had given her just before they entered the house. She felt expected to entertain the household, as well as telling the truth about the reasons for her journey, and hoped she had the storytelling skills to win her freedom among the Tlakwa. Life as a slave did not appeal to her, and she had already run from the fate of being a captive in another strange place.

Tsusiat brought her to the open hearth in the centre of the floor, where benches were pulled close to the fire's warmth. "This is Jenia don Dela don Tared," Tsusiat announced to the people gathering to meet the stranger sitting at their fire. As quickly as Tsusiat named twenty or more of the villagers, Jenia forgot their names, overcome by the strangeness of their dark-eyed, broad faces and the strong wood smoke which stung her eyes. The shapes of the women's skirts and shawls hung strangely to her eye; used as she was to woollen clothing, Jenia found the cloth of pounded cedar bark as unfamiliar to her as the soft-tanned leather of the men's breeches. She did notice, though, there were five or six other people, dressed simply and moving quietly in the corners where lamps were lighted, among those whom Tsusiat did not introduce.

Perhaps they were slaves. They did not seem cowed, or sullen to her as they worked. Some were deftly cutting up roots to put in baskets simmering in a box of hot water; others were bringing hot stones from the fire, rinsing them and dropping them into the box to keep the water near boiling. Two more quiet people were lighting stone bowl lamps. With quick, covert glances while she looked about the great wooden hall, Jenia compared them to those who had been introduced. She noticed Tsusiat stepping aside into one of the curtained alcoves, removing a shawl damp with rain. All of the people she saw looked well-fed, and the only scars she noticed were callused, workers' hands. *Well, anyone who did an honest day's work would have calluses! Even soldiers, training with spear and axe and sword, raised calluses as hard as any farmer.* It seemed a slave's life here was not as miserable as she knew it could be among even crueller masters. Their voices were quiet, but not timid under the high ceiling that echoed Talas' voice as he told of the day's boating, and how they had found nothing so memorable as one traveller, on foot on their home beach. *So this is a slave,* she thought, as a man crouched by where she sat on a bench, and asked with gestures if he could help remove her boots. *I don't need help, I'm not old and stiff, no matter where I slept last night,* she thought instantly, and it must have shown on her face. Quickly he tried to reassure her with a small smile and a shushing gesture. Gently he helped remove her boots, waved a crooked finger at her when Talas wasn't looking, and mimed carrying them away as a very heavy load. Several steps away, he sat down against the wall, and took a cloth out of an old, worn basket. He began rubbing her boots with something that looked like grease. Noticing that she was still watching him, he waved a crooked finger again and kept rubbing, but all his manner seemed to show that he was busy, very busy indeed working hard, and much too busy to be sent to bring in more firewood, when the boy beside him was sent.

"He doesn't get to do boots very often," came a quiet voice at her side. With a small start, Jenia saw Tsusiat standing beside her again, wearing a dry, woollen shawl and dry trousers under it instead of a skirt. "Most of us wear sandals or go barefoot, but some like a tough shoe." Tsusiat caught the man's eye, wagged a crooked finger at him and he shrugged, unrepentant. "He likes to tell jokes. Lema taught him to work in leather, and he'll learn how your boots were made before he gives them back."

The great wooden house was a marvel to Jenia, who had lived all her life in the much smaller, wattle-and-daub houses her folk built. There, two or three rooms would house a family, and most gatherings were held in the open square in good weather. Apparently good, dry weather came more often in her inland valley than could be expected here. *At Musky Creek, the traders built like this, too, but I didn't go indoors there.* Jenia tried not to be prying or rude as she looked around this busy place. *And they laughed when I asked when the rain was expected to stop. This is summer, it's supposed to be the dry season!*

This Tlakwa house was larger than the lord's hall she had seen in Kultis. It looked almost like a market square with a great, wooden tent sheltering a dozen partitioned stalls where families lived, and the common space. Barefoot on the pounded dirt floor, Tsusiat walked closer to an open hearth. There, red coals flared under logs as big as Jenia's leg, logs which had obviously just been added when the boats had been seen returning to the beach.

Most of the smoke went up through an open hole in the plank roof that rose more than three times her own height, but some smoke drifted among the posts and beams, and into the curtained stalls along the great plank walls. Jenia had seen whole forests of trees big and straight enough to make these beams and planks as she crossed Copper Island. She wondered how the posts were ever moved and set into place. Surely the Tlakwa would need hundreds of pairs of hands to lift those great beams, and all those people would need food and shelter for weeks while it was built. Wattle-and-daub was much simpler, in Jenia's opinion, but might not be practical here if the winter rains were hard. The bench creaked under Jenia, and she turned to see Tsusiat sitting on the other end. "Now let us have food and stories," said Talas, startling Jenia out of her quiet thoughts as he came into the brighter circle of firelight. "Let us hear from Jenia..." he looked around for a moment.

"Jenia don Dela don Tared," said one of the quiet, unnamed women as she put a bowl of soup into his hands.

"Ah! This smells good. Let us hear the story of why she is here, so we can know whether she is our welcome guest." Others came to sit or stand near the open hearth, taking bowls of soup as they were passed from hand to hand. The first row of faces was well lit by the firelight, and behind them stood other people, half-lit by lamps flickering in the shadows. The smells of smoke, of food and so many people close together pressed on Jenia like a gauze blanket, but the people were clean, the food was good and the sharp, spicy tang of the smoke was both exotic cedar and familiar enough as smoke to give Jenia a thrill as she saw the gathered people turn as one to watch her, expectantly. They quietened enough to hear as Jenia drew a deep breath to begin, fisting her hands together in her lap to keep them from trembling.

"One night very early this spring, an hour after sunset, I was suddenly no longer in my home but outdoors in a strange place where the sun was just at the horizon," Jenia began. The ring of quiet people around her murmured in satisfaction; with her first words, she had their attention and interest. One of the women dipped another bowl of soup from a cooking box and gave it to her as she spoke. "The only familiar faces I saw were my older brother and older sister, Tared and Dela. We had been falling asleep, talking quietly at home about how we wanted to travel for a while to nearby villages. We did not know where we were taken, nor for what purpose. One moment we were at home in our little house of wattle and daub, the next in this unknown place. There were many people there we had never seen before, some very strange. We were made to work with shovels and yoked pails, carrying gravel to build a road and the gravel base of a building."

Jenia paused to look around at her hosts, all of whom wore soft leather or tough cedar bark; around the adults seated on a bench came bare small children who reached, bold and shy at once, to touch the softness of her damp woollen shirt and loose pants. The threads woven in her clothes were much thinner than the wool woven into shawls or blankets draped around the Tlakwa people's shoulders.

"Many of those who worked," she said, "were dressed as though we had been taken from our beds. I was barefoot, as were most others. Some were naked, and ashamed. Others went naked and brown as if they did so all their days, but it was the labour that wore them down. And the whips. There were guards...with whips."

It was hard to talk about the whips. Jenia bit her lip and forced her hands to open, relaxing where her nails had driven into the skin of her palms. "There were guards to keep us from walking away into the forest, guards who set us to filling yoked pails and carrying them to where they were to be emptied, and these guards let the whips fall on our backs and legs if we resisted them, or if we spoke with one another, or if we simply sat down to rest. They spoke only one word to us as they showed us where we were to carry the yoked pails and place the gravel: Krummholz. Whether that was the name of the place or of the tall man who stood there, looking down on our labours, we were not told."

She was silent for a while, thinking what to say next, when Talas prompted her. "Why didn't you fight?" It seemed a natural question, hearing her story, she knew.

"We were confused, and it was dark. Perhaps the magic which the tall man made, that brought us there, also kept us bewildered." It felt like she was making a lame excuse for cowardice. She didn't want to look bad to these strangers. They were brave enough to dare the sea in their long, narrow boats. She wanted to say, *I'm not so timid, really...*

Clearing her throat, Jenia told them of one memory. "There was a man who seemed clear-headed compared to the rest of us. Naked and barehanded as he was, he grabbed a guard by her bronze armour and knocked her down. The other guards beat him to death with their boots and whips as the tall man watched and the rest of us stood with our yoked pails swinging," she said bitterly. "When it was done, the guards saluted the tall man, crying 'Krummholz!' and he told them to throw the broken body over the cliff. One of the guards fell too, but he said nothing. I've never seen a man like him, cold glaring eyes in a face that was always grim, under lank hair as bright as butter. When he walked on a ledge above us, directing his guards with a word or two and a gesture, his robe swirled as he walked and turned, swirling like smoke. Later, at daybreak when it grew light, I stole a glance over the cliff edge and saw waves pounding over rocks far below, and bones on a small stony shore. Large bones, bigger than any animal I ever saw." The soup bowl shivered in her hands, but did not spill.

"Then in the day, we were already tired and hungry and thirsty, and the whips were on our backs if we so much as looked up. But I did look up, enough to see mountains, and in the daylight the waves on the beach below."

She tried to speak with the confidence she had felt earlier, seeing the nearby low mountains against the clouds. "I saw the low mountains inland from this bay, on this island. This is where I was taken, and it must have been by magic." It sounded strange to say that word. Were the Tlakwa people more familiar with magic than her own home village? Magic still didn't seem plausible to her. "I — I didn't know magic was real, or that it made things like this happen, but nothing else could take me so far from my home in the time it takes to draw breath."

Looking around, Jenia saw she had the attention of everyone near enough to hear her, even away from the hearth, where small stone bowl lamps cast flickering lights over wooden chests in the sleeping corners of the great house. "We worked all night laying gravel for a road, and pounding it down hard, and into a shape like the floor of a building. At least," she said uncertainly, "it made me think of a building, when we were made to put a kind of wooden fence around it. And in that frame, we had to put iron bars. Were they supposed to be like tent poles? I don't know why they weren't wooden, then — some of the bars were already rusting, eaten out by the rain and the salty air from the shore."

Her audience traded knowing glances, and Talas made a crumbling gesture with his hands. "Iron is eaten by weather, here on the Island," he said. "Only copper and gold and bronze stay hard here. You know that already, do you?"

"I learned it that night and day I worked here," Jenia said wryly. "My earrings rusted through, and fell as I tried to catch them. These new ones are ruined already." She pulled her cropped hair back from one ear to show the stain of rust at her earlobe, and the crumbling ring.

"When the rain stopped at noon, we were made to mix a cold porridge of gravel and sand and powder that made Tared cough, and pour it into the double fence and onto the gravel we had pounded flat. That was when it began looking like a floor, and a set of walls that we had been building. But I didn't think of that till later, when I was travelling here, when I saw other ways of building houses and halls and barns. Then I was only carrying pails of the gravel porridge, and worrying about my brother Tared coughing as he mixed. I couldn't see our sister Dela anywhere, and didn't worry for her till later. I don't know why I wasn't thinking clearly about her when I couldn't see her. I've been tired before. It wasn't that." Her face flushed, and she hoped that was hard to see by the firelight.

"One pail spilled on him, from chin to his bare feet which were cut by the sharp, broken stones, and he was not even allowed to wash in the sea. The sun was out then," Jenia said, eyes faraway, seeing the bright sun on water after the rain had stopped, not the dark and smoky walls of the Tlakwa house. "The muddy porridge dried on him as he mixed more, and the dust made him cough as we worked. He coughed all day. There was clean water in a stone casing around a spring, but we weren't allowed to drink any of it."

Her lips and throat felt dry again with that remembered thirst, and she paused to drink from her bowl. The savoury soup was good and meaty, easing a hunger she hadn't been able to feed since she left her home. She lowered the bowl and continued speaking. "As the sun touched the horizon I saw the workers leaving. In an eye-blink, they were gone, like trout taking a fly. The man watching us sent them, sweeping his arm like he was sweeping crumbs off a table, and his guards saluted him and cried out "Krummholz!" Then I was back in my home, an hour after sunset."

There was silence again as she sipped from the bowl. A baby stirred and cried and the mother stepped aside into her family's partitioned space to unwrap and soothe it, cooing nonsense words softly at the edge of hearing. "Was it a dream?" asked Tsusiat eventually.

Jenia unlaced her woollen shirt. The women among these people wore shawls over bare breasts, so she knew their modesty would not be offended as she pulled the shirt off her back to show the stripes from the whips, now healed. "Our village was astounded to see us returned with marks of the whips and our feet torn and bruised by the sharp stones, after they had looked for us all day."

"You may have been caught by a great wizard, to be his slaves and do his work for a night and a day," said an old woman, pushing her way into the circle of firelight near the hearth. She glared at one young man until he moved aside to let her by, and stepped casually on his bare foot in passing. The people she pushed past looked away, clearly unhappy at the unwashed smell rising from her faded shawl and skirt and her stiff hide slippers.

Tsusiat leaned over to whisper in Jenia's ear. "This is Karn. Please be careful...."

"It may have been in a faraway place, south where the wizards live. You don't know anything about wizards," she said scornfully. "You don't know anything about here, either. Why would you be taken here? It was probably somewhere else, far away or long ago. Or it may have been a different world."

"It was this world, and by foot and water I have come to the place where I laboured under that spell," Jenia said grimly, putting her shirt back on. Her temper flared at the old woman's words, but she fought back the urge to speak sharply to a woman older than her own grandmother. "It was here."

"How would you know that?" demanded the old woman, warming her hands at the great fire, standing so close her slippers were in the ashes. "Here we have plenty of everything we need. Do you think we steal people to do useless work? We even had one of our own young men go missing like you, but did he go to your village and trouble your people with his story? No!" she sneered. "He was a good puller on our boats trading south, he always did his work and he never bothered anyone about it. Not like you. Bothering us! How would you know if you were taken here, of all places? How would you know that it was even this world?"

"Would another world have our moons in the same phase?" Jenia demanded. "I walked north for a month, until the light lingered longer in the sky after sunset than it does in my home village. I walked west for half a month towards the sunset, to the seashore where the sun sets later than over my home village in the mainland valley. I know the mountains I saw, veiled in rain and in clear air, as I was beaten. I know the smell and feel of the wood frames I built, the same wood you use for your houses and fire. I was here, on your island but not in your village." She felt an obscure triumph, for speaking her mind without cursing the old woman or raising her voice. More than a few admiring glances from the listening people showed they appreciated her standing up to the bad-tempered harridan. Maybe they had heard the sharp edge of her tongue many times before.

There was silence following her words, broken only by the crackling of the fire, while the old woman bristled with indignation. Finally Talas said flatly: "There is no Tower here. We have not seen one being built along our shores."

"Perhaps you had better look in the poisoned lands, then," retorted Jenia, looking into the flames rather than at him, to take the sting out of her words. "On a small mountain with a spring on its slumped shoulder, overlooking a bay of the sea." Sparks raced upwards towards the smoke hole in the roof while she watched and her hands stopped trembling.

No one commented on her suggestion. Perhaps they did not think it a wise plan. Jenia sat on the cedar bench again, and reached for the last of the soup in her bowl, now grown cold.

"So, you had an adventure, and got off lightly," said Talas at last. "A few scars to show for it, perhaps, and you were tired from your work. Now you know more of road building and wizards than you ever expected to learn, I suppose. We know little of either here." He nudged Tsusiat with a big-knuckled hand, and laughed. "We go about here in our boats, not by paths except along the shores. We build no roads. We have no wizards, here, either. The wizards are all far to the south." He winked at an old man who was carving a small piece of wood. "The only wizard we have is old Karn, and even she cannot light a lamp with a word anymore, and her medicines don't work like they used to."

He laughed again, and there were a few smiles on the faces of people standing behind the old woman.

"You still came for my salves when you strained your shoulders!" Karn screeched. "Lift your boat alone next time, and see how you feel without my medicines." She pushed her way out of the circle of light and glared at one young woman, fingering her clean, embroidered shawl, greedy eyes bright, but the woman gently took the shawl from her hands and stepped back to let Karn pass. "No peace for you when you sleep without my salves," she muttered at Talas as she tottered towards a dark corner.

"I had a terrible adventure," Jenia said softly. Before her, a log burned through and fell into the coals, breaking apart with a soft thud and a shower of sparks. "But Tared had his death of that night and day's work. We found him in his bed, his tanned skin blistered from the muddy porridge, his lungs eaten out by the dust that burned him like lime for the garden. He coughed blood. He died after two days of pain." Shocked gasps met her words, and she saw sympathy in the dark eyes of the Tlakwa people. The strange spell of which she spoke seemed no longer to be a prank, or a whim, but an accident gone awry.

"And Dela, your sister — was she as well as you after you all returned?" asked Tsusiat softly, when no one else spoke.

"My sister miscarried, and lost the babe of our hopes." Jenia heard a gasp of sympathy, and another hot bowl of soup was pressed gently into her hands by the woman who had served her earlier. "Dela had only vague memories of our hardships when she recovered. Usually she remembers things very well, she keeps our home in good order and she plans our work for each day. She remembered that night and day very differently from me, insisting we were taken to help build a fairy's palace, and we were honoured to be chosen to build a beautiful tower."

One of the bare little children who had crept close enough to listen whispered, "But fairies are only in stories."

"And so were the nightmare beasts, until the poisoned highlands brought them out of the bogs," said Tsusiat. "But I think these fairies were only in Dela's dream, Lop, not walking under the two moons."

Jenia wondered if the Tlakwa people felt like she was a dream instead of a real person walking into their home, eating their food. Were they afraid of her, or did they see her as a person much like themselves? The man still polishing her boots didn't seem afraid of her. "Dela was afraid of what had happened to us. She wouldn't talk with me about how we were called for Krummholz, or how Tared died. At the funeral, she didn't want to help cut our long hair in mourning, as is proper, so I had to cut my own hair short after cutting hers. The funeral chants were miserable for both of us, an empty acknowledgement of our loss. She won't consider looking together for a husband, or for another orphan to be our brother," Jenia said, almost into her bowl as she sipped. "She even said that it was my fault. I had wanted us to travel to nearby villages after the babe was born, and they were agreeing with my wishes, just as we were taken by the magic. She said that I must be a wizard myself, and made it happen, so that we were chosen instead of someone else, stronger people more suited to build a palace."

"Some palace," grunted Talas. "Mud and broken stone, and rusting iron poles. Your Dela was wandering in her mind when she called that a fairy palace. And could you be a wizard, caught like that, like a fish in a net? Karn," he called. "Come tell us if our guest is a wizard."

Jenia relaxed inwardly, but tried to give no sign. So she was a guest now, instead of a stranger who might be thrown off the headland for lying or spying. She felt the knot of worry in her gut relax even as she heard the old woman screech, "What, you care what I think? When my medicines no longer work? If I cannot light your lamps, how do you think I can tell if she is a wizard or telling winter stories out of season?"

"Karn can tell," Tsusiat said softly to Jenia, pulling long dark hair into a braid that the firelight gave red highlights. "She has no one to train now, and is still looking. No one wants to train with her, her temper is bad since the end of winter, and her songs and dances rarely work now."

With a temper like that, it was no wonder at all no one wanted to train with the old witch. The sour thought drifted away as Jenia watched Tsusiat's hands moving, plaiting dark hair long like Dela's before it was cut for the funeral. But Dela's hands were not so long and lean. Jenia found herself wondering if those hands were strong, and if Tsusiat had any gift for easing and rubbing pains from strained shoulders. She called her mind back to matters at hand.

"I know I am no wizard," Jenia said with a sniff. The idea had hurt when Dela had suggested it, but her poor sister could not be held responsible for the effects of the magic abduction. As if Jenia would have done anything likely to get Tared or Dela kidnapped, and herself as well! O Tared, buried now, and the small bundle of our hopes with him... Jenia felt her eyes sting at the thought, and tried to talk of more practical things. "The only gift I have is for pruning fruit trees so they bear well. Often I can coax a tree others thought was dying into bearing fruit again, but that is hardly magic. I learned it from my parents before they died, and practiced with Dela and Tared for years to do it well." In fact, Jenia was very good at it, better than either of her parents or her siblings. Her grafts nearly always took, her pruning cuts rarely infected, and neighbours insisted that after she worked on the pet trees at their doors, the fruit was larger and sweeter. *But boasting is of little use, when one blight striking an orchard could ruin all the gardeners' hopes for the season.*

The child who had spoken earlier wormed his way through the adults and came up to Jenia's elbow, where he tugged on the sleeve of her wool shirt, distracting her. She was touched by the engaging, open curiosity on his grubby face. "Was that all your adventures?" he asked wistfully.

"No," Jenia said with a smile. She saw other children being given food from their parents' bowls, and knew children were well-loved here. This strange village, with only four great houses instead of two dozen huts, began to seem less strange to her. "I also pruned trees on my way here. It was like being at home in my mother's orchard, so it did not seem like a daring adventure to me, but maybe it would to you. I have not seen any orchards here."

"What's an orchard?" he asked, eyes gone round.

"It is a place where trees that grow fruits or nuts are planted together, close to a home or a village," Jenia explained. "The trees will get plenty of sunshine and rain, and you don't have to go looking all through forests of other trees to find the ones with fruit."

He nodded. "Karn grows some plants like that, by her house. She calls it a garden. Tell me your story," he said, and sat friendly and trusting on the floor beside her, petting the small white dog that had crept up unnoticed, and now lay curled dry and warm at her feet. "Tell me like Tsusiat tells me a story. 'One day under the two moons and the bright sun, Jenia came to an orchard...'" he prompted, and Jenia began.

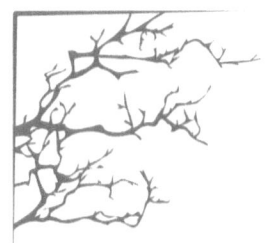

Chapter Three

"One day under the two moons and the bright sun, as she travelled on her way to your village, Jenia came to an orchard," she said smiling, and as the story spun out of her, Jenia let her awareness of the two dozen or more listeners around the fire fade so that her tongue would loosen and she could speak more easily. She spoke only to the grubby child at her feet, and it was as if she were telling him not of plain things which happened in her own life, but adventures from one of the folk stories her own grandmother had told her years ago while they shelled nuts or peeled apples. Not even two phases of the greater moon had passed since she had stepped into that old orchard, but already it seemed as though someone else had touched those trees. "She had never seen fruit trees like these, so long neglected..."

Jenia wondered what sort of orchard this was, that the fine old trees had been left neglected for years to send up suckers and steep boughs too high for any picker to reach. More than five years had passed without them feeling the pruner's knife, she guessed, touching the boughs of a gnarled Fairweather pear. Beside it grew a Red Olan apple, and in rows along a shallow hillside she saw acres of trees, neatly laid out as if with great care. But the grass grew long beneath the trees, neither mown nor grazed, growing tangled with mint and mendwell and other herbs. There was no sign anyone had passed among the trees to do anything more than pick the ripe fruit within easy reach.

There was a wasp nest in one plum tree; not a new one, but for three years or more the wasps had been building their paper nest into a spiral ball larger than a man's head. She heard it humming and avoided the carpet of windfall plums, unripe but long gone rotten in the tall grass. Only an ignorant idiot would walk under a wasp's nest in warm weather. Another tree had a slim bough broken and sagging. Jenia bit her lip and drew the bronze knife she carried at her hip. Carefully she cut off the branch at the girdle, below the break, where it could heal. Then she cleaned her knife on the grass and with water from her skin bota, before wiping it dry and putting it away.

Not even the most simple work had been done to maintain the orchard, not in years, she realized, and while some of the trees grew too tall now for convenience, others were twisting and shading their own fruit-bearing limbs. Yet much of the fruit was not lying underfoot as windfalls, rotten after winter rains, but had been picked and taken away, so she knew people still lived nearby. Why had the orchard, once so fine and varied enough to be a king's treasure, been neglected? Jenia walked on, looking for beehives or crop fields to tell her if she was coming closer to a village.

It was not a village she found at last, but a strange sort of cluster of houses behind a wall around a hilltop. A cobbled road ran up to a gate, and behind the stone wall rose several low roofs and the higher roof of a stone house. The littler houses were plain wood, and clay, but never before had Jenia seen a house made of blocks of stone.

She had laid loose rock walls in the fields of her home valley, of course, and built small houses of wattle-and-daub with Tared and Dela, plastering the walls with a mixture of clay and dried grasses. But seeing stone laid and piled like cordwood was new to her, and she wondered how it was done. It was suddenly clear to her in one turn of the greater moon's phases she had indeed walked far from her home village. Even the houses, the walls, the very stone was different from what she knew. She had never seen stone like this, fine grained like golden sand, cut and set as the cobbles she walked on and the wall she walked past as the gate opened for her.

"What do you want, young woman?" asked a man standing with the guard at the gate, a man dressed in armour of leather and bronze over his linen shirt and trousers of rough wool dyed nut-brown. "Tell us who you are."

"I am Jenia don Dela don Tared," she said. "What town have I found here?"

His eyes gleamed, tawny in the shadow of his helmet. "I am Ronay, the Captain of the Lord's Guard here. Have you come to give your services to Lord Regis and his hold called Kultis?" Looking her over from head to foot, Ronay rubbed the back of one gloved hand over the neat beard bristling at his chin.

Jenia stood inside the iron gate, shifting her half-empty pack from one shoulder to the other as she looked around the market square. She could smell a tannery and a blacksmith's shop, and a bakery in the tangle of scents caught inside the walls. "I came north from my home in the narrow valley, and now I am travelling to the west, to the seacoast," she told the Captain. *That was enough to tell him,* she thought. *He'll have no interest in why I am travelling.* "My name is Jenia don Dela don Tared. I am looking for work I can do for a handful of days, to replace my travelling provisions."

(The listening child asked, "Why didn't she just eat what she could find as she travelled?"

"Hush, Lop," Tsusiat whispered. "Some places have different forests and no beaches. And some people are not hunters or gatherers. Listen to the story.")

Ronay left the guard at the gate and took Jenia to a great hall in the house of stone, and made her known to Lord Regis. When the lord asked her what work she was able to do, he plainly expected to hear she was a weaver. "Your woollen clothes are finely made," he told the footsore young woman standing before his chair. "Can you weave a bolt of that cloth in a few days?" he asked, and his voice echoed from the stone walls of the great hall.

"I am not a weaver," Jenia told the lord, who leaned on the arm of his chair. "I am an arborist, a gardener of fruit trees, and as I came here I passed through an orchard long untended. Have you no one who cares for the trees?"

"We have been much occupied improving our town of Kultis," said Lord Regis. "We have been training soldiers and calling craftsmen to ply their trades within our walls. We have new ploughs for the fields, and hard, sharp scythes to cut the grain. Now we are becoming prosperous. Since the old gardener died seven years ago, the orchards have continued without the waste of a younger man's time. The trees still bear."

"With respect," said Jenia humbly, for she did not mean to argue, "if the trees are not pruned before they bud, they should not be cut this year. And if they go many more years without the pruner's knife, they will bear less fruit and it will be hard to pick what fruit does grow." The waste of leaving such fine trees untended seemed very wrong to her.

"The trees still bear," the lord repeated, not believing what she said. He shifted in his oaken chair and his linen robes fell into new folds. "We need clothes and grain and goods for trade in Kultis, not fruit trees. There is enough fruit already."

Something about the lord's manner of speech, a slightly slurred tone though his eyes were clear and his hands steady, gave Jenia an idea what to say next. "If you will forgive me asking," she said diffidently, "but I am wondering how many teeth you have." Lord Regis stared at her as if she had just sprouted a pair of wings and flown away to the smaller moon. "You have lost some teeth, have you not?" she asked, sure now of what would be his answer.

"Yes," he said curtly, through clenched jaws, not without a glance aside at his Captain; a glance which promised dire consequences if Ronay so much as smiled.

"Lord Regis, I have eaten fruit since I was a child. Even in late winter we had apples and pears and plums kept in storage, sound and sweet after many months." Jenia stepped closer to the lord's oaken chair that he could look at her more closely. "You can see that I have all my teeth. So did my mother, at forty-five summers, after bearing three children." Belatedly she became aware that she was standing on the carpet that extended in front of the lord's chair. She was glad her boots were clean and dry, even though they were worn and scuffed with travel.

At a gesture from his lord, Ronay stepped closer to inspect Jenia's broad smile. "She does appear to have all her teeth," he reported. Almost under his breath, he added: "It would be good to have soldiers who would be less likely to come down with toothache in the cold weather. You say eating fruit is good for the teeth?" he asked, plainly unsure of how this could be.

"All fruits and vegetables are. Why else do farmers eat cabbages and turnips when porridge and bread are so cheap?" She shrugged. "Apples take far less work than cabbages and carrots." It was plain to her at least that Ronay had either been born to a warrior clan or had left his peasant origins very far behind him when he took up the sword. It was equally plain the lord was not fully impressed by Jenia's words; he might even be inferring that if he had properly overseen the orchard's maintenance, there might have been enough fruit to eat that losing teeth might not have been the inevitable result of attaining his middle years.

"The trees still bear," he said again, smoothing his linen robe over his knees. "We have enough, and little or no time to spare on frivolous ideas like this — that is the proper domain of a simple-wife, or an idle hedge-wizard."

"Yes, they still bear, on the highest branches for the birds," she snapped. "Have your harvesters complained that the ladders are too short? Did the one who broke a bough, climbing, also break a limb as he fell?"

"Who told you of these things? Did you have time to gossip with people in town before facing me? Well, it is no real secret that Ronay is short one man in his company from that accident," the lord admitted. "Perhaps the work of pruning is worth something to us, then, if it frees our young men to have two whole legs and to be soldiers."

"Then I will work for you for a week," said Jenia, "and do my best among your trees. If you can spare someone to scythe the grass under the trees, I will teach that person to make a fine mulch for the trees in summer."

So it was that Ronay sent one man or another from among his guard to work with the scythe and learn from Jenia how to pile cut grass, wood-ash and manure in heaps to compost for mulch. "There may not be anyone free to spread it under the trees, after summer," Ronay warned her, as she cleaned her pruning knife and moved to yet another tree on the shallow hillside. "Lord Regis may send us patrolling the fields, or guarding against raiders on the outlying farms."

"The mulch will be all the better for lying longer," Jenia said, unworried. She stepped back to look at the shape of the apple tree before her, looking for a way to let more sunlight into the centre of the halo of branches. "It may be spread at any time, but it is miserable work in winter."

"And what would you know of miserable work?" he asked, amused, and scratched the big barrel of his chest inside his armour. "You have never faced a battle. I hear the farm workers singing as they harvest crops."

Her mouth opened, then closed on what she had first started to say. Eventually she said only, "I wonder if you heard them singing as they pull weeds in the rain..." She waited, but there was no answer. The captain left her then, walking along the hillside to the cobbled road that led into the gates of the city.

(The listening child fidgeted. "Is it hard to grow food, instead of finding it?" he asked, and was threatened with being sent to bed if he interrupted again. "But I want to hear the story," he insisted, and was still.)

He came again to the orchard in the afternoon, two days later. Jenia's boots had been newly shined with tallow, and hanging from a tree was her pack, now full again with waybread and dried meat. "You have been given credit at the bakery?" he guessed, feeling the pack with one gloved hand.

Jenia shook her head, keeping her balance on the ladder where she worked. "This was a gift from the baker. She said she knew because of the pruning there should be more and better fruit for years to come, and she would owe me. She wanted to give me cake, but this was all she had ready. The soldiers want only journey-bread, she told me, no sweets or treats."

"We need to be ready to go on patrol at any time," he said absently. Looking at the broad area of mown grass, he nodded approvingly. "You are getting good work out of my men. We shall have to call you Corporal," he teased her. "Where did you learn to give orders?"

She descended the ladder, and moved it around the pear tree, before saying eventually, "Oh, any farmer knows a hundred places to put a pair of hands to work." Stretching a scratched hand, Jenia looked around the grass and herbs under the trees. *Ow, this stings. Is there any mendwell around?* she wondered. *It grows anywhere —dry places, wet places, half-way up an old rock wall...* There were the feathery leaves of mendwell, up against the trunk of the tree she was working on. She crushed a leaf's juices into her scratch, then set her hands and feet to climb the ladder once more.

After a moment she sighed. "Really, Captain, I cannot work with your armour creaking behind me like that." She added lightly, as though her skin did not crawl at the thought of the armed man standing behind her, "Can you not hand me the pruning hook if you are not going to work elsewhere?"

He handed it to her automatically, then realized he had taken directions from a small woman, grubby with sap and crumbs of bark. "You're no corporal," he said. "We'll have to call you Sergeant, at least. What do they call you at home?"

"Jenia," she said shortly, wrestling with the pruning hook. It wasn't as well-made as her own pruning hook back home, with a wooden shaft her brother had sanded smooth. This long handle had been left out in the rain and the woodgrain had become splintery. "Or, 'Oi, you! Supper's ready, come down out of that tree!'"

"That sounds like a mother calling." Ronay's tawny eyes crinkled as he smiled.

"And after she died, my sister took up calling me for supper. She keeps our little house and cooks our evening meals. I make porridge for our mornings."

"You have no husband to call home for his meal?" Ronay tucked the frayed cuff of his linen shirt under his glove.

"None yet," she said, climbing a step higher on the ladder, looking at the branch she was trimming rather than at him. "None I am looking for, yet. After I travel to the seashore and then return home, my sister and I will need to decide if either of us needs to find a husband more than we both need to find another orphan to be our brother."

"You may not need to go looking. There may be a place for you here...Sergeant." He laughed as he walked away along the long rows of trees back to the gates of Kultis.

AT THE END OF THE WEEK Ronay came again with the young soldier working as the grass-mower, to bring Jenia her pay, a heavy bag of iron nails generously measured by his own broad hands. His helmet and sword were left behind at the wall, there being no need for them in the orchard, and his gloves with them, but he had not taken time to remove his armour. Jenia wondered if he slept in it — he certainly didn't remove it to clean the leather and felt padding very often. She suppressed the ungraceful thought as she accepted her pay.

"Lord Regis is well pleased with reports of how you have spent your time here, and wishes for you to complete the entire orchard," the Captain told her, tawny eyes meeting her grey eyes as their hands touched for a moment on the leather bag. Then his hand slid around hers, supporting the weight of the bag. His calluses felt smooth and hard, not rough like a farmer's hand. "We want you to stay. There — there is a place for you here," he added in a rush, and for a moment he seemed to be waiting for her to answer, but she didn't know what he expected.

It would be an impossible task this spring, Jenia had to explain. The trees were budding already, and most of the pruning should wait until the leaves fell. But he didn't seem to take her objection seriously.

"I am charged to tell you Lord Regis wants you to trim every tree in his orchard," said the Captain of the Guard, and behind him, his soldier swung a scythe, mowing tall grass in methodical, tired arcs. "But what I wish to tell you as well is that there is a place for you here ... that I wish to ask if you would consider—"

"Don't—" Jenia started to call out to the mower, but thought better of it. *Let him go on the way he is,* she decided as her temper flared. "Every tree? Some are saplings, in the new ranks, and overcrowded. They need no pruning, but thinning."

Ronay waved one hand, his armour of leather and metal creaking. "We can cut down any sapling you choose," he said easily. "My soldiers can call it axe-training. Look how well they handled the mowing you've had them do."

"But you don't just cut them down," she protested. "Some of the branches can be grafted on to other trees, here or in other orchards. They're not just kindling for the fire, they can be sold.... " Her voice failed.

Ronay was nodding. "You know Lord Regis wants things of value for his hold. By coming here, you have reminded him fruit is valuable in winter, and what is too much for one town can be sold in another. Now we have learned even the cut branches can be valued."

Jenia's hands tightened on the small, heavy bag. "I have to leave now. I have a journey to make this season. I can stay no longer."

"You will stay," the Captain said in a voice like the cutting stroke of the scythe, slow and steady. "You will stay till Lord Regis' great orchard is put to rights."

"Years of neglect cannot be made good in a single season," Jenia protested. "A few weeks of hard work in the spring, and again in the fall are not enough. It will be a labour of years, not days."

It appeared Ronay was aware of that, and was learning an orchard was not a battlefield, for it seemed he was trying to speak as gently as he could. "Then you will be the Tree-Tender of Kultis in service to Lord Regis, as respected as the weaver and the blacksmith, with soldiers to assist you."

"With soldiers to guard me," she corrected him bitterly. "And to keep me from leaving the hold as freely as the weaver and the blacksmith." She was right, for he nodded. There was not much gentleness in him, though he tried.

"You cannot leave while we need your skills so much," he said. "You will be paid well. You will have friends here, the baker and others. A fine young woman like you will soon be courted and have your choice of who to marry. In a few years it won't matter so much...." Was he trying to reassure her? "No one will be cruel to you, not if I make you my—"

He was interrupted by a horrifying screech, and the *thunk* of the scythe as it bit into a plum tree. Jenia cursed the grass-mower for an ignorant idiot as he ran towards them at top speed, shrieking.

"Well, he can't have taken his foot off if he's running like that," was all Ronay said before he was caught flat-footed and unprepared as Jenia swung her heavy bag of iron nails and hit him as hard as she could, across the bridge of his nose. He went down like a stunned calf being slaughtered.

She hadn't known it would be so easy to knock him down. Never in her life had she hit anyone like that. It was shocking, to feel the crunch and see blood spatter, but she hardened her heart even as her hands shook. She was not about to let herself be made a prisoner. Blood leaked around his hands clapped to his face, and Ronay gasped for breath. He rose to his knees for a moment, wavering, and was knocked flat by the frantic man who fell on top of him. The clatter of armour and wild howling kept either man from noticing Jenia run like a deer to where her pack and cloak hung from a low branch. She knew what was causing the soldier such distress and she needed to escape before the Captain could wrestle and kick his way clear of his man to learn for himself.

"WASPS!" The man shrieked like a loon. His Captain soon found armour was not sufficient protection from this invading army, and that being temporarily blinded with a crushed and bleeding nose made retreat difficult. Both men fought to escape the cloud of angry wasps, running into each other and several low branches in their desperate flight, and by the time calm returned to the orchard, Jenia was long gone.

Three times during the next twelve days Jenia saw Ronay and ten soldiers pursuing her westward as she bought supplies in villages with some of the good iron nails she had earned. Once the soldiers even passed beneath a tree in which she had hidden. But they did not see her, and she evaded them at the seacoast, buying passage on a trader's boat to Copper Island. And so she was not made their prisoner, and her adventures on Copper Island began.

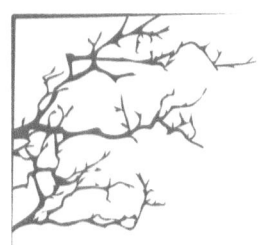

Chapter Four

A great murmur of voices rose in applause when Jenia finished, and she felt truly welcomed. Her bowl was gently taken from her hands, again, and filled once more. This time she was given fish and boiled roots to eat, and an unfamiliar fishy grease for dressing or gravy. It was very hot and very good, and Jenia found herself hungry enough to eat it all. There was plenty for everyone, she noted, and while no one crowded her from the bench near the fire, she ended up sharing the bench and its cushioning fur with Tsusiat.

"We had one young man disappear, perhaps like you as Karn said," Tsusiat said, eating roots and licking grease from clean, brown fingers. "But we never saw him again. He disappeared from the beach, not from his bed like you. We found his tracks going half-way along the shore, and stopping in mid-stride far from the headland or the water."

"You don't think he went swimming, and was lost?" Jenia asked.

"We don't think so. He certainly knew how to swim, and wouldn't have tried it there. He was a good puller, one of the strong paddlers who work in our boats you saw, and was preparing for a long trip. He wanted to travel," Tsusiat said wistfully. "He would have gone south with the traders soon, but instead we sent word south of the strange way his footsteps stopped in the middle of the beach."

If she hadn't been taken from her bed and returned just as mysteriously, Jenia wouldn't have known whether to believe this story or assume it was a fanciful tale to tell around a winter fireside. But with her own experience in mind, she began to wonder where the other people had come from to labour alongside her, building that strange construction of gravel and mud slurry.

"WE WILL SEND YOUR STORY south with the traders," Tsusiat added. "I will go one day soon and tell them your story to carry south. There may be people in far southern cities who know what happened to you. Or there may be those who will want to know. And at any rate," and here the brown eyes were wide, catching the firelight in a merry twinkle, "It will make a fine tale to tell at every fireside along the traders' route."

"You may stay with us as our guest." Talas came to sit on the next bench, a wide wooden bowl held in one hand. "Camping under the trees is hard without a good bedroll, or shelter. And there are not enough caves when it rains."

"I want to explore the island," Jenia said, looking from one to the other. Were they children of one mother? There was certainly a likeness in their faces. "There's a mountain I saw, and when I get nearer I'll recognize some of the trees. They were twisted..."

"Karn tells us there are places where the trees are twisted, but you should not go there," Talas said severely. "The poisoned bogs not only twist the trees, there are strange beasts coming out of them now. We do not go there. There are no trails, and the hills and mountains are steep."

"That sounds like the place where this work was being done," Jenia said.

"No one builds there, it is too far from the places where food is gathered. Are you so sure this is the island you seek?" Talas asked, adding more gently when she frowned, "Maybe you were mistaken."

"I know the mountain I saw before the clouds closed in. I left bloody footprints there, and I remember the crooked trees rising behind my brother Tared as he stood in clouds of rock dust that blistered him and killed him." Hands clasped around her empty bowl, Jenia looked down. "I know the well casing where my sister Dela was beaten for trying to dip her dust and sweat-stained hands for a drink of water."

"And you think it was here?"

"I know the smell of your trees and the misty rain here. Look, my bag of nails is rusting already."

"Are nails all you have brought?" Tsusiat teased, waving a crooked finger, but the gibe had no sting of meanness.

"I've brought my knife," Jenia said quietly, and held it out for them to see. "It hasn't rusted. A bronze pruning blade that has been put to good use already on my journey. I'll bring back a branch of that twisted silver wood from the bogs to lay on Tared's grave, if I can."

In days to come, in good weather, Jenia walked along the beach with the older children. She saw much of the nearby area with them, walking south one day along the shore of Home Bay to a small point of land before the smaller Sandy Bay, where they caught a fish and roasted it on a beach fire and then came walking back home. North along Home Bay was the headland with a narrow path to the top. The path forked part-way up from the beach, where another trail straggled through the trees to a beach both flatter and more open to the waves coming in off the open water. Here behind a tough hedge of springy bushes was a little house where Karn sat blinking in the sunlight, on a bench with her back against the wall.

"She can look right over her garden to the path, and see if anyone is coming," Jenia said to Lop, who was carrying a new basket carefully in both hands.

"She looks every day to see if anyone is coming," said Lop. "But we don't come every day." The new basket was set down on Karn's bench with a soft thump. "My mother has sent you a basket," said Lop shyly, before running back to Jenia's side. "Come, come! The tide is as far out as Sometime Rock, and the beach here is wide enough to play with sticks and a ball. Can you make us a ball?"

Another day the children took Jenia through the meadow behind the houses, climbing Over-the-hump of a narrow hill on the far side of the village to Reeds-and-frogs Pond as she gathered berries and greens. She was gently discouraged from walking farther inland than the first set of hills. "Bears live here, and worse," the older children told her. "Sing! We'll drive them away. They can smell us coming, and might think we're hunting unless we sing."

Tsusiat disappeared for three days in one of the long boats, with half-a-dozen young men working as pullers, but Jenia hardly noticed as Lema coaxed her into turning her pack inside-out and letting Lema handle every inch of it and of her oiled leather cloak. *Dela knows more about leather than I ever bothered to learn,* she fretted. Somehow she remembered details of how they were made for her, as Lema asked question after question about how her people tanned leather of various animals.

While Tsusiat was gone, Talas began making crab traps. Jenia watched him finish three from start to finish in the time other men took to make two or one. His big hands were deft enough to tie sinew around bent green-stick slats, but he didn't make a tiny trap like one man made for a toy. His traps were bigger than many, partly because his hands were bigger. "I want big crabs to come to my trap," Talas told Jenia. "Little ones are allowed to escape." He would not let her help, or make her own trap, saying that wasn't proper for an unmarried young woman; but he let her watch and asked her to bring him cool water to drink as he sat working in the bright sunshine so the sinew would dry tight.

She brought his big, wooden cup full of cold water from the stream, and he thanked her before drinking it all. "Some of the traps are different from others," she said. "Look, the one he's making is like the first one you made, a square box. But this one you're making is round on top and bottom, with straight sides. Do they catch different crabs?"

"Not really," said Talas, pulling another knot tight. "I have never had a round and a square one at the same time. I want to see if there is much difference besides the round one being a little easier to make."

"Did you learn how to make them from your father?" she asked.

"My uncle taught me the square trap. Macu, there, makes them like turtles with flat bottom and humped top. It was Tsusiat who made our first round trap."

That baffled Jenia for a moment. "But you said that it wouldn't be proper if I made one. I'm an unmarried young woman."

"No, it wouldn't," Talas said lightly, tying off the end of a sinew and taking up another as he spoke. "It is one of the things we expect people to know, but you didn't grow up here."

"So why could Tsusiat make one? I'm sorry," she said in a rush. "I don't mean to be rude. There's a lot I don't understand about what people are expected to do or say. Is it because Tsusiat is your—"

"When I was a boy with my first boat," Talas said, interrupting her, "I was supposed to be watching the little ones. We were on a beach, three coves along that shore to the south, not shallow like our home beach but one that goes deep suddenly. I thought I was watching them all well enough, but our little sister came and told me Tsusiat was swimming."

He pointed out at the horizon. "See the clouds coming up, like hills and mountains? It was the same that day. Tsusiat wanted to swim to the land that had come to visit us. By the time I ran to my boat and paddled out from the cove, I could see only a little, dark head bobbing in the waves. Tsusiat was very far from shore when I got there, and very cold, and said the water was singing...." He tied another knot and yet another knot before speaking again. "That day changed Tsusiat, or maybe that was the first we saw it. Many of the things we expect people to do or not do — we have learned Tsusiat will not always do what we expect," he said, with a sad smile. "And for Tsusiat, that is proper. At least it was for our mother, and for Karn, and for our little sister who is gone."

He took up a last strand of sinew. "The round trap is a good one, but we don't make many of them. If you would get one of the children to bring me water, I would be glad to drink again." Jenia knew to go then, and found Lop to go running with Talas' wooden cup.

The clean wood smoke smell of the great wooden house was in Jenia's hair and clothing, as much as any of the people who lived there. She hung her clothes in the wind to blow fresh, and bathed in the river, but each night as the biting insects closed in, she was grateful for the smoke which took its time about escaping through the smoke hole in the roof.

Karn seemed unaffected by them, often sitting outside for long evenings by the village houses as the sky grew darker. She watched the stars wheel in the sky and mumbled to herself. Jenia didn't know what to make of her songs.

Tsusiat had even more songs. Old ones, new ones from this latest trip, one that named every pool in the stream that ran through the meadow, beside the houses and into the sea: Big Wash, Big Rinse, and Little Rinse, and above the ford were Crayfish Here, and No Wading Broken Pots. "Lema's first husband broke her dye pots here," Tsusiat said. "Then he went to live in Opitsat. She has new clay pots to mix her dyes. And a new husband now."

It was Tsusiat who showed her how to wade in the shallows of a narrow cove on the low headland's rocky shore between Home Bay and Sandy Bay, wading on sand gone white with broken seashells to find oysters bigger than her own two small hands. They scrambled up the rocky shore to a grassy, dirty shoulder of land a few feet above the shore of the cove. There Tsusiat pushed a few blackened rocks together and lit a small fire that settled into a bed of red coals while they talked about a bank of fog approaching, almost hiding some rocks a stone's throw offshore. Seals would bask there on bright days, but Jenia couldn't see any today. A simple bench made from three boards of weather-silvered cedar was tucked under the cove's little bent oak trees, a bench bigger than one person needed and just big enough for two. *Did Tsusiat bring it here a few winters ago?* Jenia wondered, but didn't ask. *Maybe Talas or someone else brought the boards here and knocked them into a bench while waiting for a fire to burn down into coals. How long has the bench been sitting here?*

"If we're going to make oyster soup, or dry them, we usually shuck them on the beach and throw the shells back into the water," said Tsusiat. "No, we don't need your knife for that — it's hard on a good knife. Look what we'll do instead...." The big oysters were set over the coals, and when the heat had steamed the meat inside, the shells opened.

Nothing had tasted so good, salt and tangy meat, not since Jenia left behind the foods of home. "Thank you," she said, to the mindless oysters that opened themselves for her. She looked out over the water as waves receded along the shoreline, glad to be here in this moment and happy enough for now to take her time learning to find her way around the shores of this island. "Thank you," she said to Tsusiat, who seemed strangely shy when they were done eating. Tsusiat gathered the empty shells and tossed them down the grassy slope, past the rocks to the white beach.

The sand along the bay was grey, Jenia knew, but this little cove was white with hundreds of seashells laying in the shallows and all through the small stones of the beach: shells like bowls or matched like left and right hands, and whorls that spiraled round like snail shells. "Moon snails and whelks," Jenia said. "The children have been teaching me. Clams and oysters, and...." Her voice went dry. The shells from their meal lay there, a large double handful, and she began to see this little cove as armful after armful of shells similarly cast back on the shore.

There were hundreds of whole shells, and uncountable broken ones as well, not only where they had been wading but out to the rocks. The whole cove was white with fragments of shell. When she and Tsusiat had slogged up the cove's beach barefoot with hands full of oysters, their footprints had gouged deep scoops visible from where she stood, deep footprints that revealed more white shell pieces. Stepping to the edge of the grassy shoulder of land, Jenia stared down into swaths of white shell fragments that slid away into the dark depths of the water as waves washed in and out. These were shells from thousands of meals, for untold years beyond grandmother days. There were crumbs of shell in the dirt under her feet. She'd never seen time so clearly before, not one wave and another one and another, but a sequence that built as simply as raindrops over immense time.

"We like it here," said Tsusiat.

THE NEXT DAY WAS FOGGY but with a bright overcast. The weather changed so much here that Jenia couldn't tell whether or not it was going to rain later. Jenia was splattered with wet sand on the tidal flats, playing with the children, when a band of soldiers came Over-the-hump of the low hill and across the meadow to the shoreline. If none of the dozen soldiers recognized her, half-clad and muddy as Tsusiat or the children building sand villages, Jenia recognized their leather armour and greaves, and she fled. Shedding sand and mud as she went, Jenia ran for the nearest of the great wooden houses, where there were many of the Tlakwa people. She would not stand behind children when Ronay recognized her. She already knew him, by his uniform, and by the slant she had put in his nose under the rim of his bronze helmet.

This meeting of strangers did not go so well for the soldiers as they seemed to expect. Only their captain spoke, and he said the same things again and again. "We are charged to bring her back to Kultis," Ronay told the Tlakwa men and women gathered in the questioning place on the headland above the village. There were three or four dozen people, Jenia saw, and more coming up the footpath from the houses. "We have orders from our Lord." Somehow without any orders or directions that Jenia saw, every villager was standing between the soldiers and the only easy path down the headland. When a wave broke hard on the rocky shore below, Ronay turned at the sound of the water crashing and sucking back between the rocks, then faced the villagers again.

Talas said flatly, "She is our honoured guest, and not to be turned over to you like a hunted thief or a criminal."

"She stole away talents our Lord wants to contract and to pay for fairly," Ronay insisted. Jenia saw his eyes flicker as he took in the steep cliff to one side and behind him. It was clear he was not comfortable standing between the Tlakwa people and the cliff's edge. "She left two injured men behind her, and we demand restitution." He stepped forward a little, then back, with one hand resting on his sword in its sheath.

"We have heard that story before, of how your Lord's men do not know enough to leave wasps alone, and we heard of a merry dance with a bag of nails." No smile showed on Talas' face, but his tone was no longer solemn. He waved a crooked finger at them, and finally Jenia could see it was a sign of humour, and a warning not to take one's self too seriously. It was clear he was unafraid of the armed men standing on the headland above the village. "If you are so thoughtless and clumsy, how will our friend be safe travelling with you? You have not even a boat to bring her by."

"She'll come back with us the way we came," Ronay blustered. "We'll cross the island and hire a boat on the other side."

"How many of your fighters did you lose crossing the bogs in the highlands?" Tsusiat asked then. "There were more of you when you started than the eight who stand here in the questioning place. No, I didn't hide in the trees and watch you secretly, but I can see there's peat and mud on your greaves, and one of your men is carrying two packs. That woman — did she leave Kultis carrying two swords? I think you lost at least one of your soldiers in the poisoned bogs, to the strange beasts there."

Some of the soldiers made warding signs where Tsusiat could not see, but Jenia noticed, and saw at least one of those hands tremble. Their captain did not appear afraid, though. "We have a right to take her with us," Ronay insisted.

"No right that is recognized here. We have called her guest and friend. We have not called you the same." Now Talas spoke grimly. The edge of the cliff seemed closer behind the soldiers who stood together.

"We will not fight such peaceful, honest people for her." It was plain to Jenia Ronay was reaching hard to find within him the role of diplomat. He scratched at his neck, where old welts from wasp stings were matched with new marks that looked like the bites of the little flying, whining insects hereabouts.

"That is good, for there are many more of us at Opitsat and other villages. You would not leave our island again."

"We will leave the way we came."

"Cross the forbidden ground again and we will send words to those who ferried you across in their fishing boats. They will not carry any who are spared by the poisoned bogs."

"Then we will hire the use of your boats, to return us to the mainland. After we have convinced Jenia to return with us." Ronay set his jaw, and his whole manner challenged Talas to disagree.

"You may have the pleasure of attempting to convince her," Talas agreed easily, and to the Captain's evident surprise. "I would suggest that fine stories and gifts will make a good beginning, as Jenia tells many stories herself and has but few plain possessions in her pack."

A flush rose quickly up from Ronay's collar. "I'm not here to court her for marriage! I'm taking her back to work for a living. Honest work," he added quickly. "For good pay, and respect from a good lord."

"I do not think you will convince her. But so long as you do not steal her away, or beat her or frighten her into leaving with you, you may camp at the edge of the meadow near the beach, and make your petition." Talas stretched his long arms.

"Do not be long-winded about it," he added. "Summer lasts long here, but the winters are cold and wet. You will need more than a tent for your comfort after the equinox, when the storms come."

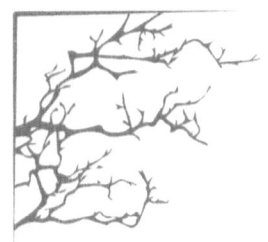

Chapter Five

As day was ending, Jenia slipped out of the big house where the door was propped open, leaving her cloak and pack behind. She ran for the beach, then slowed above the tide line where grey sand dragged her footsteps. The tide was very high, and swept along only yards from the winter-tossed logs that were silvered with sun and rain, faintly visible in the dusk by starlight through patchy clouds. The greater moon had not yet risen.

This was pointless. Her whole search seemed stalled and pointless now, and by coming to Copper Island she had brought danger to these quiet people. If the soldiers were not willing to accept her refusal, or to back down when the Tlakwa people defended her right not to be captured, there would be fighting, she was sure.

The memory of the one fight she had ever experienced was upsetting and brought a sour taste to Jenia's mouth; she remembered the sickening crunch as Ronay's nose broke and the fear that lent her speed to run far away before the wasps were done with him or his clumsy soldier. The memory sat uneasily on her heart. Even childhood scuffles with Tared or his friends had always left her feeling sick and angry, but back then she had always been the one who lost the scuffle. She had not lost to Ronay, if anyone ever won a fight.

She wished she could think better of herself. What was the difference, now, between her and the guards with whips who had beaten her and other cowed people under the calm, ruthless regard of the wizard? *Krummholz!* She thought like a curse. There wasn't enough difference for her to be proud of her virtue, she knew. She too had dealt out pain and suffering that was unexpected.

The waves pounded in against the shore as she walked, foam luminescent in the faint light from the sky. Underfoot she could see nothing in the dusk, and tripped over kelp and driftwood as she walked. Out from under the trees, the open space around her seemed immense, extending out over the ocean like a bowl, but the shoreline and meadow rose like a dark wall, hemming her in along the beach. There was only a narrow track for her to run easily along, and under that wide open sky she felt trapped between the slight bluff and the water's edge.

Maybe it was time to leave, now, on her own. *I could cross the island again; I've done it before. The bogs couldn't be that hard to avoid,* she told herself. *It's not like anyone sent me to go there or wants me to find that wizard. Nobody needs me to do anything about him. Even Dela said she didn't care when I told her what I planned to do. Just come home when you're done, was all she said.*

She should leave and take the soldiers' interest away from the village. She should flee before they could bring her forcibly back to Kultis, that strange walled village with a gate that locked people in as much as it locked invaders out.

She should run from these villagers too, who worked as hard as any field hands ever did, collecting fish or roots, but who rested instead of planting or tilling, and who even yet did not understand the desperate intensity of her search. Why search for an evil place? Why go looking for a man all sensible people would avoid? They would never know, and every day she spent in these warm meadows and cool waters would cool her resolve.

It was time she left. She felt the frustration gel in her, and resolved that she would leave, but not by the inland route, near the bogs. In the morning, she would continue her coastline walk of the island till she had gone right round it, climbing headlands and even cliffs if necessary.

It was at that moment that she felt the sand fading from beneath her feet. But it wasn't the undertow of the surf pulling sand away — it was a disorienting whirl that made the greater moon just rising and the lesser moon high overhead spin in a crazy dance around her. When it settled, the greater moon was half-way up the arc of the sky, with no clouds to dim the stars.

The roar of the waves was gone. She whirled, and lost her balance, falling full length on stony ground pounded hard and dry by many feet. The first breath she drew had no salt or seaweed tang, but bore instead a dry, dusty smell somehow familiar. Jenia turned her head, and instead of trees towering above her on the headland, she saw the leather and bronze armour she had seen before in the night and day she had laboured on the strange building. The scent of a soldier's sweat came to her then, striking fear into her heart without clearing her head. The cut of his whip brought Jenia to her feet with the speed that was necessary to avoid a second blow, as she remembered to her shame.

There were others, bewildered as she, driven into ranks shuffling across the small, cool stones pounded into hardpan underfoot. A basket was pushed into her numb hands, and by the time Jenia could think clearly she had filled, carried and emptied it several times. She'd been walking into a gully and filling the basket with small, hard stones, and carrying the basket out of the gully over to some kind of table to empty it, then back to the gully without pause. Had hours passed? The ache in her shoulders and arms said so. Next to her, a little man old enough to be a grandfather hitched up his shirt and limped along with a basket. *He shouldn't be so sad,* Jenia thought numbly. *The wrinkles in his face are from smiling. Poor man.* Other workers used picks to pry stones from the wall of the gully, and Jenia and the old man scooped them into baskets with their hands.

The greater moon stood overhead and the stars had moved to different places by the time she was made to give her basket to another worker, a man more frightened, numb and bewildered than she. He wore only a swath of linen wrapped around his loins, and his bare feet were bleeding already. At least I have my boots this time, Jenia thought, dimly remembering being barefoot on cruel, sharp stones.

Jenia and others were made to sort baskets of stones others emptied onto great wooden frames like tables with screens for tops instead of boards. She and a boy, younger than she but with shoulders like an apprentice smith, shook one of the screens over another basket, putting stones larger than her own small fists aside into a separate pile. The nearest guard struck them both with a gloved fist, and pointed at a lump of clay stained with iron ore among the stones. That was to be tossed aside, was the clear message.

Jenia learned quickly, and the boy seemed disposed to work as earnestly here as he must have at home. Lumps of iron-stained clay were thrown aside underfoot. Stones that were small fell through the screen into baskets; these baskets of small stones were hauled by shuffling, grimy workers and dumped on a heap growing nearby. Big stones left on top of the screen were tumbled into baskets that were hauled to a different heap.

But resentment boiled inside her as Jenia found her head clearing. Through the dawn and the long day while she worked, she had time to think as she kept her hands working. She could see the punishment for resting or resisting being meted our around her, and had no wish to earn more than the few cuts from the whips which had already come her way.

But she did not wish to be as meek as she appeared. She couldn't fight the guards, or flee them — and where would she run? This stone quarry was in the middle of an open, rolling prairie of grasses from shoulder-high down to ankle-high, with not so much as one tree for miles around, as far as she could see in any direction. But even if she couldn't run, she would not merely submit to the whips and the cold stare of the man standing above them on the edge of the quarry.

"Krummholz!" the guards called and saluted with their swords, and as Jenia saw their faces turned away, she put clumps of the iron-stained clay among the sorted stones. Again and again she did so, whenever possible from morning through the long day, hiding the lumps under loose gravel when she could. A few workers around the frames noticed what she was doing, and sharing sidelong glances, followed suit. If the guards and Krummholz wanted the clay taken out, she would put it back out of rebellion.

Sometimes the clay was seen by the casual glance of a guard, and blows rained down on one or more of the workers. But Jenia persisted, and by the end of the long day she took a perverse pride in the knowledge that every basket of stones she had sorted had at least one lump of the iron-stained clay hidden in it. She had no idea what iron or clay would do to the gravel porridge when it was poured at the tower site, but if she had been told to sort out the lumps, that was reason enough for her to leave them.

What good a hill of small stones would do anyone here on a prairie's grassy knolls, she had no idea. But if Krummholz could bring and send people by his magic, Jenia supposed it was equally probable that he could move stones. With scant experience in magic up to this season, it was remarkable what abilities she was willing to attribute to magic.

"I haven't even seen Karn light the lamps by saying a single word," Jenia grumbled. Straightening her stiff back, she caught sight of the sunset colours, gold and orange in the dust streaming downwind from the gravel pit. The stamp of booted feet approaching, and a guard's barked order made Jenia flinch and turn swiftly back to the screen; gawking at the sunset could earn her a blow from a heavy fist, or worse.

When the sun stood half-sunk below the horizon, level as the ocean Jenia had seen from Copper Island, the workers were made to leave their baskets and screens and stand together near the mound of sorted stones. On the edge of the quarry stood Krummholz, his raised hands pale where the sleeves of his grey robe fell back. His butter-yellow hair grew dark with sweat as his brow furrowed in concentration. Jenia blinked, and the hill of stones was gone. Krummholz lowered his hands, a look of satisfaction now apparent on his face and in his stance. A few moments later, he waved a hand almost casually towards the mass of his assembled workers, who began to fade much more slowly than the stones had.

Jenia had time to look to her left at a whiskery youth with hands scraped raw and bleeding who went slack-jawed and dull-eyed as the wave of magic swept upon them. His whisper, "I only wanted to leave home for a while," made her shiver, and she looked away to her right as the woman beside her began to slump, dead before she fell. The man behind her cried out, "Home, I want to be home! And I swear I'll never wish to leave it again..." as he faded from her view.

I can't go home yet! I haven't done what I came to the island for. I have to go back there! The hardpan stones faded beneath her feet and became the loose, yielding surface of dry sand, above the high tide line on the Tlakwa's home beach.

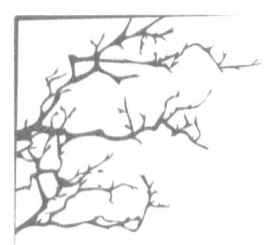

Chapter Six

"I don't know where I was taken this time," Jenia said, looking into Tsusiat's calm, brown eyes to see if she was believed. The confidence she found there gave her courage to go on, and to speak louder than the waves pounding at Sometime Rock, that only showed in this shallow cove at low tide. They sat on a bench made simply from a plank balanced on two short logs, but the plank was chiseled and sanded as smooth and comfortable as the dovetailed benches in the village's big houses. Together they leaned back against the outer wall of Karn's little house. The wall's rougher cedar planks were weathered silver as beach logs, even though the house was sheltered from the offshore wind by a sturdy thicket. "But I think it was the quarry from which Krummholz brought the gravel for his tower and the road from the bog. The stones were the right size, and the right colour — dusty brown tones, not the dull grey of stones near my home village, or white-grey of the beach sand here or the black of the headlands here."

Karn came out of her house with a wooden box in her hands, full of branches of dried herbs. She shoved Jenia over on the bench, and sat beside her, groaning. When a bundle of herbs was thrust into Jenia's hands, she summoned up all the patience she could and tried to sort the tangle as Karn was doing.

"So that is where you spent yesterday. We thought you were up early, wandering, when your bed was found empty. That's what Lema said you did some mornings, while I was away. And so the Tower is still being built," Tsusiat said thoughtfully. "By the same methods — stones and dust brought by magic, and workers too, who are not fed or housed or given any care by this wizard's power."

"Wizards don't always care," Karn grumbled. Her hands kept moving, busy as a knitter, fingers sorting dried leaves from the tangle of herbs in her lap. "But the ones who remember where they came from pick up after themselves. When great power comes some wizards forget kindness is another strength.

They call up armies for great battles, and spill their blood like winter rain. Only the gentlest of wizards remembers to heal his tools, but the strongest never care to bother."

Karn is neither strong nor gentle. Jenia kept the thought to herself. *What sort of wizard is she supposed to be? Back home, I'd call her a bad-tempered herb-woman.* Travel had taught Jenia the value of keeping her opinions to herself. It was an effort sometimes, but this time she managed to keep her lips closed. It wasn't any easier when Tsusiat winked, smiling at Karn's strident tone, and waved a crooked finger when the old woman wasn't looking.

Karn stretched and groaned. "My hands are aching. It's going to rain soon."

For a while, they sorted herbs in silence, stripping dried leaves from stems. The leaves were put back into Karn's box, and the stems put to one side on the bench. The waves were quiet on the shallow sand when Tsusiat spoke up. "In the south, the traders have heard of great battles. I was taught a story of one battle."

"Can you tell it to me?" Jenia asked. To her surprise, instead of remaining seated on the bench, Tsusiat rose to stand on the sands of this small cove over the headland from the Tlakwa home beach. Back straight, breathing deeply, Tsusiat's gaze went unfocussed and turned strangely inward. As the story began, it was not told lightly and naturally as Tsusiat had been speaking until now, but chanted. The words were spoken in subtle rhythm, and four times a verse was repeated.

> *Ai, ai, and the gulls wheel round*
> *the broken tower on the chalky land*
> *the river drained will fill again*
> *as it drained from his broken hand*

It was not the sort of story Jenia was used to hearing, of one hero's adventure or one traveller's journey. When armies assemble and do battle, there ought to be a story for every pair of feet marching. But in Tsusiat's tale, there was a name for the chalk hill above the meadow where the armies met, and for the milky river that ran red that day, but no names for any of the fighters. Not even the wizards were named: neither the one who defended a tower nor those who won the day.

"Another tower being built," Jenia mused, when Tsusiat was done. "And a battle when it was found by other wizards. Maybe after I find this tower, I can lead other wizards to it. I wonder if other wizards are any better company than this one."

"I wonder if they are any easier to find." Tsusiat took another handful of the herbs to sort and sat again on the bench, warm against Jenia's arm and side.

That feels good, realized Jenia. It had been a long time since anyone touched her at all. Most people greeting strangers didn't even touch hands. Leaning a little into Tsusiat's warmth felt good. *I wish Dela didn't blame me for our losses, Tared and her lost hoped-for babe. She never used to hold a grudge, not when I was a child underfoot and she my big sister who taught me how to sharpen our mother's pruning saws. I wish she'll still want to make a home with me when I come back, when I've solved this search for the wizard. She did say she wanted me to come home safe. I wish I knew for sure whether I still belong there.* She let the thought trickle away.

"I wonder if wizards know how to fight without armies dying for them," Jenia said. "Krummholz doesn't do his own work; he steals away people to work for him. I wonder where he got the guards, and if they were cruel before working with him." There was a thistle tangled in Jenia's handful of herbs, scratching her. She tossed it aside and sucked on her finger. "It doesn't sound like a wizard is someone confident in personal power, if a wizard has to raise an army to do the fighting. Look how much Krummholz gets done with a handful of guards. What would he do with a real army?"

Tsusiat shrugged. "Maybe the armies are mostly a distraction from what is really happening, from the real battle." The offshore wind was blowing more strongly now, as the waves crested low on the beach where the tide was turning and beginning to rise.

Jenia had to think about that idea for a while. A bank of dark, towering clouds was moving in from over the open sea. *It is going to rain soon,* she knew. *Karn was right.* "What else could be happening, but hundreds of people dying? Isn't that what happens in battles?"

"Maybe not to wizards."

"In that chant, were the wizards more interested in the tower?" she wondered.

"And in the hill, and the river that looped around it." Tsusiat put dried leaves into Karn's box and bundled the bare stems between hands fragrant with oils from the herbs. Small green shreds and dust fell, dancing motes that disappeared as the sunlight faded. "People come, people go very easily, sometimes leaving no more behind them than a bird does flying across the sky. It takes time to bend a river. It takes time to make a hill or wear it down."

The first raindrops pattered on the beach and thicket. A smell came up from the ground that was good to Jenia: last year's leaves lying under the thicket, green leaves and wet bark, black earth under the little trees, white-grey sand going dark grey under rain spattering to beat down the edges of their footprints into anonymous dips and curves.

"I had better find this tower first, before trying to figure out how to bring other wizards here to break it." *I won't get there in this morning's rain, that's for sure,* she knew.

"I wouldn't worry about it," said Karn with a sniff. "Fretting here, running there, going where you don't know what to expect. You don't want to be facing those odd, twisted beasts in the bogs."

"So the creatures find and follow people who walk inland, then?" Jenia asked. "Are you willing to tell me more? It seems they're not just bears, or stories to keep little ones like Lop from wandering away from home. Why didn't they find me when I crossed the island?"

"They don't find me either when I go inland for my herbs," Karn said with a sniff. "I bathe three times in the cove, sing my gathering song, and put on fresh clothing hung in the off-shore breeze for a day before I walk inland."

Jenia couldn't see what good singing a song or ducking into the cold ocean water would do to keep away either story-beasts or real animals. *Maybe it's a ritual that gives her confidence. Or maybe these beasts in the bogs really are mostly just stories, to frighten children and keep people away from more ordinary dangers, like getting mired or drinking stagnant bog water. There might only be a very few beasts.*

"Come inside, out of the rain," said Karn. "This squall will pass before long. You can make me tea," she said, with an air of conferring a great favour upon both her visitors.

"Tsusiat, I've been wondering." Jenia paused in the doorway to Karn's little house, silvered outside with weathered wood but dark inside where Karn was fumbling to light the stone bowl that was her lamp. "How can there be standing water in the highlands of this island? Or a spring where I saw it, on the shoulder of that low mountain? Water runs downhill."

The offshore breeze turned cold, and Tsusiat shivered, urging her indoors. "You saw the great mountains on the mainland coast, on your journey, with snow on their peaks all through the year. Those mountains are many times higher than this island's hills. The snow melts on that high rock, and runs down into it, pressing down under the strait and pressing up into our island rock."

"Water passing through rock? And under seawater?" Jenia was in the dark, unsure where to put her feet among Karn's wooden bins.

"It is a mystery," Tsusiat agreed, surefooted in the dim room. "Karn followed one of our springs in a dream, all the way to the high mountains on the mainland and back. It took her a night and a day. I remember wondering if she would ever wake, but just at sunset she did." The scents of wood smoke and dried herbs rose as Tsusiat brushed past Jenia in the dark "The bogs are different from the springs. They come from rainwater standing in rocky hollows, pockets lined with rotting peat, so it cannot drain away. The waters do not mix. It is another mystery. We would know nothing of how such things happen just by looking and walking past," said that warm voice out of the dark. "It took Karn to follow the springs, and her grandmother to see inside the bogs and tell what she saw to her sister, who was my mother's grandmother. Here, Karn, let me light the lamp and the fire. I'll make the tea. It will do us all good."

The rain lasted only an hour, and left the air clean. Karn tottered out to the shore to set out fishing lines twisted from cedar roots, and Tsusiat went back over the headland to the village. This was a good time to walk inland a little ways, Jenia decided, and come back before she would be missed. She didn't want to offend anyone by breaking the rule against going inland, even if Karn could do so. It was easy to walk away with no one seeing her. Tall trees came right down to the shoreline at Karn's cove, and her little house was under their spreading branches. The tall trunks rose like pillars to the canopy of branches high overhead, many times the height of a tall man.

It's higher than the roof in Lord Regis' hall in Kultis, and grander, Jenia thought. Her newly-oiled boots were cushioned on fallen fir needles, rusty-brown and still almost dry after that rain, carpeting the ground under the tall trees. She brushed past pungent herbs like kingsfoil where there were spaces open to the sky; she smiled to find the feathery fronds of mendwell like a dear friend, and wondered what to call another herb, something minty that had prickly flowers instead of soft white buds. Despite the kindness of the Tlakwa it was time for her to go looking again for the twisted trees, to find the place where something was being built by magic. She'd waited long enough on the shoreline. That odd-shaped mountain lay somewhere inland, and she meant to find it. Somehow she would understand what had been happening, and what she should do. She headed uphill and inland.

There was no bog over the first ridge of hills, but the next peak was higher, with smaller trees. At this hill's crest Jenia paused, with grass and herbs under her boots. Goldwort grew here, tangled around a tree stump, and she stroked the glossy, crisp leaves. It was good to see familiar plants just then, where so many growing things were different from her home valley.

The tree she stood beside was a fir, not tall and straight like those on the low ground. Here, on higher and stonier ground, the trees were stunted to only twice or three times her own height. There were not only conifers, but a few broad-leaved trees as well, oaks and another type with peeling bark, here where the sun was able to shine in through fewer boughs. *I should keep on learning from Karn and Tsusiat the names of all these trees,* she decided. *That really is proper learning for an arborist, to be a scholar of trees. And how the Tlakwa people use them, as lumber for their great houses, or making crab traps like Talas does. There are trap designs he said he would show me...* One tree had peeling rusty bark like she'd never seen before, but the one she leaned against was a more familiar oak.

At least, judging from the bent limb she rested her hand on, it was. Jenia took a second look, and saw the clusters of pine needles at the end of the bent branch. This was no oak tree, with a gnarled branch. This was a pine like she'd never seen before. She looked at it closely, tracing out the contorted limbs bent like arms at wrist and elbow. Even the grain under the bark must be twisted, she knew. *This isn't the disease which sometimes afflicts maple trees.* That one produced a thousand tiny branches starting under the bark, and when the wood was sawn and planed right for lumber, the *bird's eyes* made the grain strikingly beautiful. This was a twist as if soft new branches had been bent at right angles and tied there, to grow crooked and thick over time. Jenia could see no marks of wires in the bark. This tree had grown misshapen with no hand to guide it.

There was another nearby, with stunted branches winding around the trunk. A third bore one limb at the base and but two more eight feet higher. The trunk in between looked straight until Jenia came close and laid hands on it. Then she could make out by the bark that the entire tree had a complete twist in the middle.

Jenia didn't know what to think. Her eyes and her hands told her that no pruning knife had been laid to these trees, but there was something familiar about the tension in the limbs. She remembered a pear orchard in a neighbouring village near her home, where all the limbs hung down in great, black arcs from the trunks, while the year's new growth shot straight upwards, stiff as the quills on a hedgehog. She shuddered, remembering those trees that no child would play under, and thought deliberately instead of her own dwarfed apple trees, grafted branches rising not even ten feet from the ground. Just as those branches had been carefully trimmed to let in light, and to push up and out at a strong angle, these trees had been twisted and stunted purposefully. Her own apple trees were tended pets, growing strong limbs like Tared's muscled arms and legs that had stretched and bunched and stretched again, loading and unloading carts for market, stronger every year until he coughed his life away. But these twisted pines were not rising to stretch in the sun, turning sunlight into apples for joy. They were cripples.

The ground shifted under her feet, spongy and damp. The sky was open above her head, no canopy of tall trees, and only a few tattered clouds now the rain had blown past. She moved on, avoiding pools of standing water rimmed with moss and low, scrubby plants. Sedge sprung up in grass-like tufts, and feathery mendwell's pungent tang rose from under her boots. *Even mendwell's scent that clears the nose and throat of racking coughs was not enough to save Tared,* she remembered sadly. She'd crushed the leaves and washed the juices over his blistered sores, and made teas for his bleeding mouth, but nothing had made him breathe easier. As the sun came out from behind clouds and the day warmed, some of the plants sparkled with great sticky drops on sparse green spines. The sweet scent made her drowsy as she crouched, and when she rose, the buzz and drone of small bog creatures faded as she approached. The frogs and crickets took up their song again behind her when she moved on through the bogs.

There was a white tree, partly visible through the scrubby brush. She edged round one deep pond, watching the great white pitchfork of a tree become visible as her boots suddenly grated on gravel. Underfoot there was a path of small stones pounded together. Jenia stopped.

The frogs were silent behind her. Turning, she saw Ronay and two of his soldiers across the deep pond. Instantly she ran, away from the soldiers and the gravel path, across the spongy ground where her feet made deep marks.

They've been looking for me, she thought. *Trying to find me away from the village, where no one will know if they catch me and take me with them.*

Pushing through scrubby brush, Jenia could hear them cursing as they followed more slowly. Anyone could follow her tracks on this wet ground. She moved faster, slipping on rough rock and wet moss that she hoped would slow her hunters more than it did her. Scrambling along a fallen log, she stumbled at the tangle of its roots into something that was warm and furry.

A snarl brought her to her feet. Jenia leapt sideways without looking, fighting to keep on her feet as the touch of fur silky as a cat faded from her fingertips. She landed in water to her knees, not knowing which way to run.

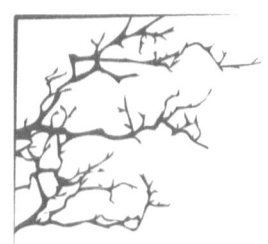

Chapter Seven

Jenia stood rooted, unable to move as her feet sank into the peaty muck. Only after the beast snarled and shifted its furry coils in her direction did she realize she had not even considered fleeing towards Ronay and the soldiers. But by that time they were already in motion.

Ronay passed her, so close the great steel sword he carried whistled as it cut the air right before her face. His left hand jabbed out, signaling one soldier to move to his left, and she did so, her own weapon in hand. The beast hissed and darted its clawed tail at that soldier, who did not flinch. As she met the blow with her blade, Ronay and the other soldier faced the fangs.

Jenia knew this was her moment to move, and she drew her feet out of the peaty muck, lucky not to lose her slim boots. She stumbled back, turning away from the beast. Out of the water, she staggered onto relatively dry ground, looking around for a rock or a tree branch, but nothing came to hand. She heard a shout, an unfamiliar man's voice, and Ronay answering, saying, "Back, Tanner, and to your right!" Movement a step behind her brought all her cropped hair up on end, and she shied away from whatever was approaching. But it wasn't the furred beast striking like a snake; it was Ronay's armoured shoulder striking her as he dodged. He cursed her for being underfoot, and humbly she scrambled further.

Oh, the shame of it, hindering him while he fought and protected her! No rocks to throw, no branches to swing... Jenia drew her pruning knife and turned to face the struggle. *Maybe I can't fight like a soldier, with a sword. But if a loop of those shifting coils gets past Ronay and close to me, I can prick it like a boil.*

The beast yowled, striking with tail at one soldier and jaws at another, as the length of its body stretched and writhed over fallen log, ground and bog indiscriminately. If cats hated water, this beast took no notice as the woman soldier pinned its clawed tail under her sword's point in the muck. If snakes were cold, the coil that looped past Ronay's thigh and groped towards the woman was hot under Jenia's hand when she darted forward and struck with her small knife. She leaped back quickly, not wanting to crowd Ronay. *He's fast, for all that he's big. I never saw him fight before, never knew he was so fast.* As Ronay moved in and struck, then faded back out of reach, he seemed to know where his soldiers were moving, even while watching the beast's swaying head.

Should I run? It's not as if I'm really helping here, she thought desperately. *They shouldn't have to look out for me as they move. They shouldn't have chased me, they ran me right towards it! But they didn't have to fight it, either.* Numbly, she realized that it would have been easy for them to run, to let the beast take her while they got away.

The younger soldier darted forward, to strike at the long neck beside the whiskered head. The bronze sword glanced away. His boot slipped in the peaty muck underfoot, as the furred jaws dropped open and venom jetted from the beast's slender fangs. He shrieked when the smoking drops fell on bare skin at his wrist, but Ronay was already swinging his blade through the beast's extended neck. The head fell, still snapping at the soldiers' feet, and the beast's body slumped and flailed.

Ronay pulled the groaning soldier away from the dying beast. The man's bare arm was already welting up from the poison. Fumbling with a water flask, Ronay turned, looking for Jenia. "You! Do you know medicines for poison? Herbs?" He poured clean water over the younger man's welted arm, trying to wash away the beast's venom.

Still trying to run, Jenia hesitated. They had defended her from the beast, and now this man's face twisted in pain, while she stood numb and useless. Jenia looked around, only her gaze moving at first, and then her shaking hands as she wiped her pruning knife and put it away. She stepped away from the beast's writhing coils and pulled up a feathery clump of mendwell. It was the first herb that came to hand, and she'd walked past clumps of it all day. And goldwort was growing against a stump, just two steps away. She forced numb feet to carry her forward, and trembling hands to strip glossy leaves from the twisted vine.

Something brushed against her leg, and she leapt away from a coil of the beast, still hot and still moving. The beast was headless, she told herself, and as the woman soldier slashed away the spiked tail, Jenia knew it couldn't hurt her. She dared to approach the beast, knowing to fear it no more than a duck still struggling after its head was lopped clean away. But it was harder for her to come near the cursing soldier and Ronay with his blood-streaked sword. Even the other soldier still held her sword in both hands, and was turning warily, looking into the bog and the dark under the trees at the edge of the forest for other dangers. All her senses were still on alert. *The fight is over,* she realized. *But why am I still afraid?*

"I know a poultice for bee stings, or hornets," Jenia stammered. "But I don't know if it works on snake's poison."

"Get over here and make your damned mess of herbs," Ronay snapped. "Are you afraid I'll catch you and bind you with a rope? Not just at the moment." The bleeding stump of the beast's neck flailed against his knee, and he kicked it away, scattering blood drops over the moss, brighter than red maple leaves in autumn.

Wanting to trust him, Jenia came closer. She began chewing the goldwort leaves, careful not to swallow their bitter milky juices, while between her hands she crushed the mendwell leaves and stems. Working the two pulped plants together, she made a green salve that always before had reduced the swelling and itch of beestings. It worked quickly on this man's swollen welts, but did little for his pain.

"So you know what to do for bee stings," Ronay grumbled, while Jenia racked her brains trying to think of what people did for pain when there wasn't any willow bark. She hadn't even seen any willows on Copper Island. *What sort of people don't grow willows?* she wondered. *They don't even make wattle-and-daub houses, or bentwood chairs. This is what comes of not growing willows. Only hard benches to sit on in houses as big and as hard to heat as a market square, and a man groaning on his knees in swamp water, and not one of us with so much as a whistle, let alone willow bark tea for his pain.*

"It strikes me that you might have stayed around for a while in the orchard, and told me what to do for wasp stings," said Ronay. There were still marks on his wrists and throat where he had been stung and stung again by the swarm. "Or this bend you put in my nose."

"Captain," said the soldier, standing guard over them all. "Something's moving in the bog, just out of sight past those scrubby bushes. We should move out of here, back towards the shoreline, before it finds us."

All of them were on their feet in an instant, even the soldier cradling his arm. He stopped moaning, and took hold of his sword again. No one wanted to see what could come out of the bog. If it were cat-snake or bear or only a weasel, they would leave it behind.

They clambered up out of the rocky hollow that cradled the bog, over the crest of the hill, stumbling on rough rocks and bent roots of scrubby trees. "Twisted, unnatural beast. That's one hide I don't want for a rug." Ronay spat into a stream as they crossed it, coming down the slope of a ravine and up the other side. They pushed on together through straight, tall trees over the crest of another hill, and eventually found a way through scrubby underbrush that was hard to push aside, but had no thorns.

The sight of open water below them seemed to clear all their heads of the fog and stink of fear. As they reached a moss-covered headland, high above the waves of an unfamiliar beach, the soldiers took time to clean and put away their swords. The swelling was definitely going down on the young man's arm, but he winced as he flexed it, watching the fading welts twist over corded muscle. "Hurts like a brand, Captain," he said. "But I can use it."

Ronay nodded. "You see, we need what you know," he said suddenly, and Jenia realized with a start that he was addressing her, not the soldier. "We work better together than apart, in truth, and we'll leave this island better together than if we fight, or if I dared bind you and risk the wrath of your village full of friends."

"I don't want to travel with you," Jenia said. "My business is here."

"I don't see what you can think to do on a rock where it rains half the time," Ronay growled, exasperated. "Are you still afraid of an orderly, regular life inside walls? Or is it this you fear?" He indicated his breastplate, mud-stained greaves, and helmet. "I see you've put aside your bag of nails, so I must learn not to fear you any further, though I tell you I still am of a mind to look for wasp nests when I pass under trees." His attempt at humour didn't warm her, and he abandoned it, saying seriously: "You don't have to fear me as if I wanted to hurt you. I have much to offer for you — an honest, honourable offer. There is a place for you —"

"You haven't listened to me," Jenia insisted. *And every word he says,* she realized, *frustrates and baffles me. It sounds like perfectly normal words, but whenever he talks he's not really answering what I say or believing what I tell him.* "I'm not leaving with you. I'm not even going home yet until I search this island. I know where I'm going. It can't be far. That mountain is one I remember," she said, pointing. Ronay turned to look, and with the change in his balance, the moss under his boot heel slid. He fell to the rock with a thump and clang of bronze.

Jenia took her chance without a second thought and darted away, light feet seeking narrow footholds in the rocks, too narrow for Ronay's broad boots. Over the rocky edge and down into a bay she hadn't explored, clambering without looking ahead, Jenia found that anger gave her daring if not the speed of fear. She was down at the edge of the waves almost before she knew it, and the scrabble of hard leather and armour against the rock told her that the others were close behind her. The waves pulled back from the shore for an instant, and Jenia darted across a gap, leaping between wet stones draped with green and brown seaweed. Then the waves surged forward, as she leaped onto a rock shelf. Behind her came a cry, almost smothered in the crash of a wave.

"Tanner's gone under, Captain," said the woman soldier. "Give me your hand!" This to the man struggling in the white foam, who appeared not to hear her.

"Take my rope," Ronay was saying, as he pulled a coil of hemp cord from the small pack at his shoulder. The woman soldier had already dropped her sword and helmet at his feet, and took the end of the rope from him and wrapped it around one hand before he could say more.

"I'll bring him out," she said confidently. "I can swim." She stepped off the rocks, saying, "It isn't deep here, see?" as another wave struck.

"Marta!" Ronay barked after her, paying out line while taking firm hold of the rest of the coil. Jenia left them to their rescue and clambered to higher ground as the wave came up onto her rock shelf. When the water pulled back, Ronay was shouting again, and she turned, balancing with hands on barnacled rock wet with spray.

Both soldiers were being pulled away from shore by the undertow, and as she watched the line was torn from Ronay's hands. He stumbled forward, stepping into the shallow water which now covered the rocks Jenia had run across, but he could not grasp the rope before it was out of reach. And it was clear to Jenia that both soldiers were drowning, even the one who had said she could swim. Their armour held them down in the cold water, and the undertow pulled them back against a rock twenty feet from shore with a head-cracking *smack!* that made Jenia's teeth ache where she clung, just within the spray of the next wave.

This one almost took Ronay off his feet, but he kept his balance and got one hand onto the rock shelf. Jenia retreated farther, climbing, as he pulled his attention away from his drowning soldiers for a moment and looked up for her.

"You — lured us here!" he snarled. "You witched up the waves to take Marta and Tanner. Are you water-witch now, too, as well as trickster and tree-witch? You've put some kind of spell on me to make me want — " His grip failed and he let out a surprising *yip!* as he made a desperate grab for the rock.

His voice and the pounding of the waves were echoing strangely over her head; Jenia looked around and up to find that she'd retreated into a seashore cave, and was scrabbling along the high tide mark. At least, she hoped it was the high tide mark. There was no easier exit farther along the shore, only a sheer cliff.

"I'd bind you with a rope, now, if I still had one," Ronay swore, and he crawled up the rocks after her. "Be a captive then, if you're unwilling to take good offers and do as you're told. I don't know why I ever hoped you would see reason and take my offer, or my lord's offer. I've spent the lives of two good soldiers making you my prisoner, instead of my —"

"I am not your prisoner, Captain," she interrupted him, loud enough to be heard above the pounding waves. "We are both captured by the sea. It will be hours before the tide goes out enough to let us pass the way we came." She and Ronay were trapped together in the sea-cave.

"You lured us here, so the waves would take us," he accused her.

Jenia shook her head, climbing up the rough shingle past what she thought was the high tide line. "I've never been to this bay," she told him, scrambling away as he tried to close in on her.

"You trapped me here, to work your magic on me and turn me against my duty," Ronay insisted. For all that his strides were long, he lost half the ground gained with each step as the loose shingle slid away underfoot on the steep beach. It was a hard climb for him to reach the narrow strip of level shingle above the tide line. "You witched my mind, and made me believe that I wanted you for my own.... You make a fool of me with your magic."

"What magic?" Anger and fear boiled together in her. "Are you a plum tree, that I can coax blossoms out of you? Shall I tie you to a south-facing wall and bring ripe fruit out of you two weeks earlier than your brothers in the orchard?" Her hands shook, but her voice was steady. "If I had any magic, Captain, I can tell you it would not be used to bring you anywhere near myself, nor to trap us together here in the cold wind. I would send you home to patrol your walled town, leaving me alone in my search."

"What could you be looking for here?" he demanded. "Gold? There's hardly enough of that here to be worth your stubbornness. There are other islands with more. If you were a metalworker or a miner you'd be looking for copper here. What is it? Some magic herb you farmers keep secrets about? For pity's sake I could help you find it and return with me. I can count leaves or pick flowers as well as anyone," he said with a shrug.

Judging from the fact Ronay hadn't recognized even mendwell trampled pungent and aromatic under his boots in the bogs, Jenia wouldn't have trusted him to weed a row of beans. "I am not looking for herbs," she said shortly. "I am looking for a tower of gravel and rock dust, poured together wet to set like — like cold porridge sets in a pot."

Ronay turned his gaze towards the approaching tide, trying to judge how high it would come. "There's no tower built here, among these wild, ignorant people. And towers aren't made like that, they're built from wood or blocks of stone mortared together."

"I know what I saw as it was being built," Jenia said. "It was the base for a broad building that would be very high. Looking at your walls at Kultis helped me understand what was being built. I hadn't thought of homes or sheds or barns that could be so big until I saw the Tlakwa village. These people aren't ignorant, they just live differently from how people do in your village or mine. Not everybody builds the same way, or talks the same way. You say plenty of things I don't understand even if you use the same words. I don't know why anyone would need a tower, or any building so large and cold, but that is what was being made when I was there."

"You worked on a stone tower?"

"With my brother and sister, and some two hundred other unwilling workers." As briefly and dispassionately as she could, Jenia told Ronay of what had happened.

"There are supposed to be wizards and their towers in the far south, if stories are to be believed," Ronay said after a while. "How do you know your tower wasn't there? How could you ever find it?"

For answer, Jenia looked up and around, as if she could look through the walls of the sea-cave. "It's on the shoulder of a low mountain I saw here twice in the last few days, when the fog burned off and the clouds cleared. There are several of those twisted trees at the worksite where Krummholz has poisoned the bogs. I found trees I recognized at one deep pond in the bog near where we found that beast, in particular one tall, white pitchfork of a tree. And I found also a wide, level path covered with gravel where workers could carry pail after pail of bog water to the worksite, as I did. Nearby I'll find the tower and the casing we were made to build around a spring. I'll find them either by going around the shoreline, cliffs or no cliffs, or by searching the bogs."

The wind was drying Ronay's frayed linen shirt and wool trousers, and for the last hours of the afternoon the sun shone into the sea-cave, warming them a little. The tide rose higher, waves thrashing through the tangled off-shore rocks and pounding the cliffs on either side, but Jenia thought the water would not rise so high as the weathered logs tossed high against the back wall of the cave by winter storms.

Ronay drew his sword and dagger and laid them and the leather sheaths on a log in the low sunlight to dry. He removed his armour and laid it on the log too, but Jenia thought it would take a hot, sunny day to dry out the felt lining. When he took a whetstone from his small pack and began to sharpen his dagger, it was clearly for her benefit. He was careful to be seen, and to emphasize the length and sharpness of the weapon.

Jenia had a whetstone of her own — and she didn't need to deal with the coating of rust that had already begun to stain the Captain's blade. It didn't take as long for her to test and sharpen the edge on her bronze pruning knife as Ronay took with his dagger — but then, he was working with a triple-edged blade. *A wicked-looking thing, that dagger,* she thought. *It has only one use.*

Jenia put away her whetstone and took up a piece of driftwood that lay at her feet. The wood was weathered silver outside, but the grain was still red when she whittled away long shavings. So this was how the local wood felt under her knife.

"No wonder you're afraid of me," Ronay said after a while. "The only time you've seen armed soldiers in your life they were such cruel guards, who beat you. I'm not surprised you were afraid of me."

"That's not the only time I've seen them. I saw them again, not two days ago. And rather than learning from them to fear you," she said wryly, "I learned from you how they expected me to work so that I wouldn't need to be whipped much to get a day's labour done."

"Two days ago?"

Jenia nodded. "I was taken by magic again. Far away, this time, to a wide rolling prairie without trees. We were made to dig and sort stones for the building. It was in a wide hollow, a pit dug into the level ground, and as we scraped the hollow wider we filled up baskets full of small, broken rocks. We were made to sort the gravel into heaps of different sizes."

"Another work crew with you, and the guards again?" Ronay looked thoughtful. His whetstone slid smoothly along one edge of his dagger. "And you say the wizard was standing above, looking down on you all in the gravel pit. Marvellous ideas this Krummholz comes up with — work crews that don't need to be fed or housed or tended to keep them fit to do the next day's work. I wonder if he has a business on the side, hiring out mercenaries?"

"You wouldn't want to work with him," Jenia said with a shudder. "The big ones like you are beaten especially hard, or muffled in hoods." *Tared wasn't big enough, or mean enough, for the guards to fear him,* she realized. *That's why they didn't pull a hood over his head. That's why he breathed so much of the lime dust that made him cough. Poor brother. He might not have died if he'd been big like Ronay...but they might have beaten him harder. Oh, I don't know what to think.* "Even the guards look strange, almost bewildered like the workers sometimes. I don't think they're much more content with their lot, even though they are the ones with the weapons."

"What are you making?" Ronay asked after long minutes had gone by, and it was clear she was putting more attention to the work than just aimless whittling.

Wordlessly, Jenia held out her hand, with the figure of a bird roughly outlined in the cedar: apparently it was none he could recognize or name. "Some kind of small bird," he said at last. "Is it asleep or dead?"

It's a woodpecker, you simpleton, have you never looked up when you hear one knocking on a tree trunk? She bit her lip, willing herself not to say what she thought of his ignorance. How he ever managed to track her from Kultis to the coast was beyond her. Why had he even bothered? She took it back and resumed carving. "That depends on you," she said after a while.

Late into the night, after the light was gone from the sky and when the waves curled up not ten feet from where they huddled behind the slight windbreak of the beach logs, Ronay stretched, rubbing his arms as if he were chilled. "It's growing colder," he said. "I propose a truce."

"What sort of truce?" Jenia couldn't see him, but she could hear him move a little on the shingle, dry seaweed crackling as he shifted his weight. *In this sea cave, it's as dark being inside a pocket,* she thought.

"We will be warmer if we lie close together."

"I will not lie with you," Jenia said flatly. "Don't try sweet talk instead of force, it won't work on me—"

"That's not what I mean. It's too cold to stay awake all night, waiting to see if you sprout a pair of wings and fly away before the tide goes out. We need to trust each other."

"I will not lie down in the dark with a man, especially not one who threatened me."

Sighing, he protested, "I am the same man who fought the bog beast, and killed it to protect you."

"You are the same man who said he would bind me with a rope if he still had one."

"Yes, I said that," he admitted. "And now I say this: I swear not to make you my prisoner. I swear I will not take you by force or guile. Tomorrow I will go to my camp with my soldiers, and not try again to find you alone. For now, I offer to let you come close enough to share our warmth, and only that. You had a brother, even though he is dead now. Wasn't he someone you could trust? Did you never fall asleep, huddled with him to keep warm?"

The memory of Tared struck her then, unbidden: his scent of salt and bitter willow wands, the whistles he taught her to make. "We lay back-to-back in the wagon when our father was driving home from a May festival in the next village," she said.

"Then put your back against mine as if I were your brother, and we will be warmer here. That is, if you will swear not to use your magic on me."

"I have no magic, and would not wish to use any on you."

"Fair enough." He was quiet while she came closer and patted a hollow in the stony sand, then lay down and carefully leaned against his back. After a long while he asked, "Are you planning to keep polishing that carving all night?"

"Is your armour going to smell like this all night?" she snapped. "Really, Captain, don't you have anyone to look after you? My sister never lets our clothing get so rank as your armour."

He laughed a little. "I had a servant. One of the soldiers, who looked after my gear and so on. He was the one who broke a leg in the autumn, falling from a tree in the orchard. I never got around to choosing a new one yet."

It was warmer, leaning against that back broad as a barrel, and gradually she relaxed. *That feels good,* realized Jenia. It had been a long time since anyone touched her at all. Most people greeting strangers didn't even touch hands. Leaning a little into Ronay's warmth felt good. *I wish Dela didn't blame me for our losses: Tared and her lost hoped-for babe. She did say she wanted me to come home safe. I wish I knew for sure whether I still belong there. I wish I knew whether I can really trust Ronay. He speaks so strangely sometimes, as if he expects me to understand him like we grew up in the same village telling the same stories....* She let the thought trickle away. Starlight wasn't enough to make out more than their dim shapes in the cave, but the foam on the waves glowed as the tide rose, crested and began to fall.

It was when she noticed that neither of them had spoken for a long while that Jenia realized that Ronay had fallen asleep. The tide was dropping, and as she waited the way over the rocks to the headland became clear. She left the bird carving next to Ronay's sword and dagger. Let him decide if the bird was sleeping or dead. Let him decide if he had failed in his duty and fallen asleep long enough to let her escape, or if he had trusted her enough not to fear whether she stayed or left.

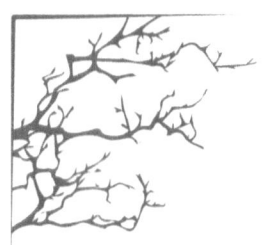

Chapter Eight

There was someone singing on the beach ahead, one bay this side of the Tlakwa village. Jenia could hear the voice, carried on the wind, but not the words. Could that cracked and hoarse sound be Tsusiat? She pushed through the springy bushes along the shore and saw that it was Karn instead, standing in her shallow cove.

Her grey hair whipped by the wind, Karn was singing hoarsely and dancing slowly as if she had been doing so since sunrise. Jenia had thought those stiff shoulders wouldn't let Karn's withering arms rise so high. But she moved easily in the morning sunlight, if slowly. In the sand Jenia saw a row of tracks left by Karn's shuffling feet, along and around a busy knot of people clustered around something she didn't recognize at first.

Then she saw it clearly. It was a whale, quite dead, being taken apart by the flensing knives of the Tlakwa women, and parts were being carried by men who joked and stepped around Karn in her dance as they carried their loads of whale meat and bone and fat. A footpath over the headland to the village was seeing steady traffic as people came and went, bowing to Karn as they passed.

Tsusiat saw her and waved, bloody to the elbows. "Come and see the whale Karn has brought us!"

Karn couldn't pull in a fishing line with a fish large enough to feed a small family, Jenia knew. How had she ever managed to catch a whale? Had she been out in a boat? Had Karn sung the whale to shore, even if she couldn't light a lamp with a word anymore? Not that Jenia had ever seen her light a lamp with anything but a stick from the fire.

Karn kept singing proudly as Jenia passed the row of footprints in the sand. Jenia bowed in respect to the old woman. *She may be stiff with age,* Jenia thought, *but she's as grand and proud as any Spring queen crowned in my village, treading out the measures of her dance on the village green at festival.* "I fed myself alone, since none would share their bowls with me," Karn sang in her quavering voice. Her wandering, cracked tune droned on as she chanted. "I filled my bowl with what the world gave me, and it was plenty. But clams did not feed all my hunger. But herbs did not talk to me across the fire. But roots and bulbs did not give my angry thoughts peace, though my belly was full when I lay down in the dark. I put out my fishing lines, and I sang for the sea to give me peace of mind and plenty. I sang even while the wind rose and threatened my small house, and even as the waves crashed and frightened me. And then I knew peace enough to sleep. And when I woke, I had caught a whale, bringing plenty to the village. Now I can share. Now I can fill the bowls of all and they will eat with me. Thanks be to the whale for coming to us..."

Jenia took her bronze knife, and undressed like the others taking the whale apart under Tsusiat's direction. Butchering a whale was very different from cleaning a rabbit or bird, or even the farm animals Jenia had butchered at home. Before long, she was as smeared with fat and blood as any of the women singing quietly along with Karn's hoarse chant.

"We thought you were sleeping at Karn's house again last night," said Tsusiat as they worked together. "But she says you were not there. Have you been walking inland on the high ground, like Karn does for her wizard's work?"

"I was trapped in a sea cave until the tide went out," Jenia admitted, both hands busy at the slippery work.

"It sounds like there is a story there to be told."

"At least one story. I know you told me the ground inland is forbidden, and you don't want me to search there for the tower." Hoping she hadn't offended, Jenia risked one glance at her friend.

Tsusiat sighed. "Karn has always walked through the high ground inland, for her meditations and to make her medicines. She is teaching you about herbs. If she does not forbid you to make your search, neither will we."

Something tense inside her untangled at Tsusiat's words, and Jenia's mind was eased. Her words came more easily then. "I was caught by the rising tide in a sea cave with Ronay. I'd been trying to run from him after he and his soldiers killed an awful beast in one of the bogs—"

"Slower, tell it slower," laughed Tsusiat. "We will be here all day, and later you can take time to tell me all the story from beginning to end. But tell me this now: was Ronay trying to steal you away, or frighten you?"

"No," said Jenia, realizing it was true. "I think he believed he was being persuasive. But he has promised not to make me his prisoner."

"Oh, so you made peace in that cave." Tsusiat's black eyes danced. "Was that all you did?"

"That was all. And it was enough."

Tsusiat stepped carefully past the fishing line that ran across the sand and under the whale's head. Jenia caught her eye, and pointed with her knife to the line. "Can you tell me how Karn could ever catch a whale with a cedar-root fishing line?" she asked quietly.

"A line like this could never tow a whale like our hunting ropes with sealskin floats, if that's what you mean." Tsusiat showed where they were to cut next, and together they peeled back a large strip of skin and blubber. "Karn has sung for peace and plenty for so long that when a whale comes to her line on the beach, we don't ask whether it came by the storm or her song. How do you know she didn't sing up the storm? She did that once, when my mother was young." Tsusiat called one of the young men to take the piece they had just cut. "It's a whale," she said eventually. "It's here and she has given it to us when we needed it."

"As if there were anything else she could do with it." The smell of blood and fat was in her nostrils, her hair — Jenia wondered if it would cling like wood sap, and stain her skin.

Tsusiat grunted. "She could leave it on the beach till it rots."

"Ooh." The idea didn't appeal to Jenia. The whale carcass was already getting a little ripe in parts, under the mid-morning sun. "I guess Karn could do that if she were angry enough."

"Takes a long time for a whale to rot away. A storm washed a blackfish whale ashore, above the tideline, a few bays north along the coast, a while back. Nobody liked using that beach for a whole year. We haven't been there yet since winter. There were good berries growing above the shoreline too," Tsusiat said ruefully. "Once you got past the reek on the beach, you hardly noticed it among the bushes and the shoreline thickets — except when the wind came in off the water. as it does most of the day. We ended up giving that beach a new name. My little cousin Lop did, the little one coming here now with a jug, when our aunt was taking us there to pick bramble berries."

"A new name?" Jenia had noticed that the Tlakwa had names for everything from portage routes around rocky streams to submerged rocks in a channel. "What was it?"

"*Please-be-bones,*" Tsusiat said, brown eyes wide as the child made a wobbly bow to old Karn and brought the heavy jug to the women butchering the whale. Watching that smile, Jenia could imagine Lop chanting those words as their long, narrow boat went around six or eight headlands to the safe but stinking harbour.

The jug was full of fresh water, very cold and very good. The women passed it around, drinking by turns, and Tsusiat poured the dregs over the head of another cousin. In the flurry of shrieks that followed, Jenia caught the jug before it fell to the sand, and gave it to the child as Tsusiat was chased around the long body of the whale and into the ebbing waves.

A movement at the edge of the trees caught Jenia's attention, and she turned to see Ronay coming out from the trees to walk along the beach. The procession was still going on, as people carrying away cuts of meat and fat took care to pass near Karn and bow before moving on towards the village. As Jenia watched, she thought that it was taking Ronay more than a few moments to understand what he was seeing. But then he bowed to the old woman, too, and made sure not to come too close to her as he passed. When he looked at Jenia holding a strip of meat taut for Tsusiat's knife, he gave her the same bow and half a smile before turning away without coming closer. She went back to her work without watching him leave.

When Jenia looked up again from her busy hands, the tide had retreated as far as Sometime Rock. The jug was in front of her again, but this time it held meat broth. She passed it to the next person, unable even to think of food while the smell of the whale was thick around her. The Tlakwa people were sharing special cuts raw, and the children were begging or snatching tidbits just ahead of the flashing knives.

There was time for Jenia to think, between the chanted songs and the work. There was time after one young man draped a cut of meat around her bare shoulders for a joke and laughed as she startled, dropping her knife. There was time after everyone dropped their knives or bundles and joined hands to dance in a circle on the beach where the tide had gone out. A whirling circle of young people stepped out from the older folk swaying in the centre, young men and young women holding hands in a ring, whipping round and turning, laughing as Jenia stumbled and caught her footing, with Tsusiat holding her up from falling in the dance. The circle spun apart into couples, men and women holding hands. One young man held his hands out to Tsusiat, who smiled while shaking that dark head a little wistfully. Instead, Tsusiat drew Jenia forward and put her hand in the young man's, fading back to stand aside from the dancing couples. The young man beamed at Jenia and led her by her smeared hands to teach her a dance step on the flat, hard sands.

There was time for her to remember both times she had disappeared for a night and a day's work that had strained her shoulders and back as sore as this day's work was doing.

But oh, how much less miserable it was to sing Karn's songs of thanks while they butchered the whale, even if Jenia did not know the words, and listen to Tsusiat tell a story of Sandpiper making dinner for Raven. How good it was to stretch and move to do another part of the work, easing cramped muscles, without a whip descending out of the dark or a haze of thirst. It was even better to take another turn dancing on the flat sands in a whirling line of young people tangling into a tight spiral and out again into a circle, with Tsusiat's hand hard in hers under the smears of blood and grease, and her other hand dwarfed in the gentle grip of one of the young men. The cedar smoke smell of the Tlakwa fires came over the headland, and Jenia would have known where she was even with her eyes closed and ears stopped up; she had walked every step of the way from her home, five hundred miles to find that scent at last. She had not been stolen out of the dark, unwilling and confused.

It was not building the Tower that was wrong, she knew as confidently as she knew how to sharpen her bronze knife. *What was wrong was stealing people to do the work, and beating it out of them with no care taken for their suffering.* How right it was to strip mine gravel from a distant prairie to Copper Island instead of quarrying granite blocks from a nearby mountain, she could not judge. Perhaps magic had its own standards which came with the abilities to go to far places and do things for which no one set of hands were strong enough.

It was not even making a good Tower, as far as she could tell, with the little she knew about building. Even if the stony porridge would set hard, surely it would break if the iron poles were already rusting. And the lumps of ironstone clay she managed to leave in the gravel would make weak spots as the clay soaked up water, swelled and crumbled. Other stolen workers, resenting the whips, would surely sort the gravel as poorly as she did. But then, perhaps magic could make the Tower strong anyway, she realized with a sigh.

The third time the jug came round it held herb tea. Jenia couldn't tell all the herbs which had been used, but there was the green of bramble leaves and the sunny scent of chamomile. She hadn't seen chamomile growing wild anywhere on Copper Island.

Just how many herbs does Karn tend in her garden? she wondered. The rumpled old witch was in her glory today, chanting over her own warm cup and sitting now on a log the children had rolled near for her. A new shawl and hat kept the bright sun off her shoulders and head, something Jenia envied. She was going to be sunburned by evening, for sure.

The whale still wasn't finished when the day was done. Jenia scrubbed at the layers of whale fat with handfuls of sand until her skin no longer felt greasy. That night she slept soundly, with a full belly and a sense perhaps the peace of which Karn sang would come again in the next day's work with the bounty they had in the bones and meat of the whale.

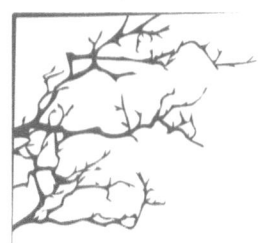

Chapter Nine

The next day, while working on the whale's carcass was a time for talking, not songs and dance. Karn tottered out with her morning tea, sitting in state again on her log in her fine new clothes, and Lop built sand villages nearby with friends running for shells and waterweeds to decorate them, and the women kept working at the whale, with knives of stone and copper and shell flashing in the grey morning haze.

The day grew warmer, and when Jenia paused to stretch she was surprised to see Ronay had come to the beach. *When he promised not to try to find me alone, did he think that meant he would watch me working with others?* She wondered. It was the first time she'd seen him go anywhere without his armour. He didn't speak to anyone, just found a place to sit a respectful distance from Karn, where his feet would not disturb the sand villages.

"You haven't told me much about your sister," said Tsusiat, both hands busy as Jenia worked to free a great bone from the carcass. "Or your brother who is gone. Don't keep watching Ronay sitting on that log in the sun. He'll get bored after a while if you stop glaring at him, and he'll go away. If he's not bothering the children, don't let him bother you. Tell me about your sister instead."

"Dela is older than I am, twenty-three summers," Jenia said, wondering where to begin. "She looks more like our father did, with hair almost as dark as yours, but grey eyes like mine and our mother. She was married for a time, but a fever came through our village and her husband died. Tared and I were glad to have her home with us again, and we all hoped her babe would be a boy she could name for her lost husband. She cooks like our mother did, she knows a hundred ways to cook apples and she can make turnips taste better than I ever could."

"Is turnip like apple? A fruit?" Tsusiat piled bones into the arms of a waiting young man, and he carried away his load toward the footpath. As he passed Ronay, the captain tugged his boots back on and rose from the log where he had been sitting, to wander away to the footpath and out of sight.

Now, how did Tsusiat know that would happen? Jenia smiled. *There are things about Ronay and how he thinks that Tsusiat understands far better than I do.* "No, turnip is a root. You don't have anything like it here. It's round, and tastes both sweet and bitter. I think that grease you put on roots would be good on turnips. When we bake ducks in clay, we pack them with pieces of turnip."

"That's how Dela cooks like your mother did," Tsusiat guessed. "She learned from your mother, who is no more?"

Jenia nodded. "Our mother was pruning, and didn't come home one evening. We found her fallen from a tree, with a broken branch. Our father was much older than she, and without her he didn't have the heart to live more than another turn of the seasons." After a long while, she thought of a question of her own. "Tsusiat, my people don't keep slaves, but we've seen them when travellers come through, and I saw more on my journey. Why do your people call them slaves, when you don't treat them badly like others do their slaves?"

"They have to work," Tsusiat said, cutting at a joint. "And they can't leave. What do your people call those who are bound to work by debt or promises or crimes, and can't leave?"

"Oh. We all work, as well as we can." She thought for a while. "And we can all leave, for a while or a lifetime."

"Then you have no slaves. Of any kind. I used to have a younger sister," Tsusiat said, and Jenia blinked, not following the reason for a change of subject. "She was going to marry a fine young man and bear heirs for Talas — you know that here, a man's heirs are his sister's children? No? Well, that is what was going to happen. But she was in a boat lost at sea last year. Talas needs a sister who can give him heirs. If we cannot adopt a sister, then I am expected...." Tsusiat worked in silence for long minutes before admitting, "I have never been very successful at doing what was expected of me."

"Brothers," sighed Jenia. "And Tared, he and I looked alike, like you and Talas, until he became a young man. He was only a year older than me. He never got as big as Talas, though, or even Ronay, the Captain of the soldiers. He was getting fine muscles from working hard. Every year he did more; he spent the last five years working as well as any man in our village. If it took trying hard, Tared could do it. At least," she added with a chuckle, "at least, as long as he didn't have to take anything apart and put it back together properly. He could never make a crab trap like the ones Talas was making the other day."

"Ah," said Tsusiat, laughing. "Couldn't build anything more complicated than a sand village? I can sing that song."

"Not even wattle-and-daub. It was Dela and I who would build a new wall if we needed it. Tared would mix clay for us to cover the walls. In our village, houses aren't big like your big houses made from big trees. Every year our little house needs a new wall, or the roof mended. That must be why he worked so long, mixing that cold stone porridge," she realized. "He was tired, and confused, and he was used to working hard, and the mixing must have seemed like familiar work. He wouldn't ever have stopped just because the dust burned in his cuts and made him cough." Her hands faltered at their work.

She stood idle for long minutes, looking out at the in-coming waves. Behind her, Tsusiat said, "We're nearly done here. You go and wash and rest. You've done more than your share." Released, Jenia ran and plunged into the shallow waves, careful not to go out too far in the cold water. There were no rocks here, but the undertow still pulled at her feet. Standing thigh-deep in the green cold, she took handfuls of sand to rub away the grease and wished, with all her strength, for the courage to be carried away by magic again. She wanted to fight the magic that had used Tared's own strength to kill him.

This time, Jenia intended not to feel caught up like driftwood on the tide. She left Karn's house as the sun was setting, saying she needed time alone on the beach to think. Karn didn't appear to notice Jenia was leaving for a walk on the beach with her boots on, with a water skin tied to her belt, and bound against her skin under her clothing, the leather bag of rusting nails.

It makes me thick-waisted as a woman five months' gone with child, Jenia thought sourly, adjusting the bag till it no longer chafed. *Good enough. If Dela could work beside me with the child in her, I can certainly bear this small, iron burden instead.* She was ready. It was time and past time to be gone from the small comforts of Karn's home, free of the clouds of stinging insects that followed her everywhere else but there or in the smoke of the Tlakwa fires. It was time she went to do what she could against the cruel work imposed on Krummholz' captives. She couldn't hide here, in the peaceful bays while the mild summer came on gently. It was time she was gone. And Jenia knew where she needed to go.

She held that thought furiously tight as she walked the beach, and hoped it would be enough to make her open to the call of magic. When Krummholz reached across farm and beach to steal his workers, his magic was like an arm sweeping a table clear of cups and bowls, but he did not take everyone in reach. He took only some. *How does he choose which people to steal?* Jenia wondered. *He doesn't take only the strongest. He doesn't take only the skilled workers or those who are proud of working hard. That one man next to me said he'd never wish to leave home again. Both times I was taken, I was wishing not to stay where I was. Is it the wish to leave that makes some people able to be stolen for his work?* Jenia knew little of magic but she held firm to her wish to be gone.

The taste of the dust that had burned Tared's lungs and killed him filled her mouth as the sand faded away from under her feet. The hard rock she felt underfoot was not grey like the sands of Copper Island, but white as chalk. Jenia felt a surge of triumph that quickly ebbed into dizziness. Her knees turned to water, and she fell to the ground, bringing her hands up to protect her head.

Under her hands, as she struggled to focus her eyes, was a seashell trapped in the white stone.

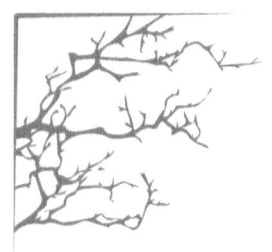

Chapter Ten

S he couldn't think, even with the drag of the bag tied around her waist to remind her of what she had planned. The waterskin was torn from her belt as she stood flatfooted, jaw slack, and a pick was thrust into her clumsy hands. Pushed by a guard, Jenia stumbled across the floor of an open quarry. She fell against someone wrapped in a loose nightshirt, who drooled as he pried rocks from the rough wall. The guard moved on as they put their tools to use without speaking.

Jenia worked an endless time breaking chunks of the white stone from the walls of the quarry, chunks that other workers were made to pile and carry away in baskets. It must have been hours later, for the stars had moved overhead when she dared to glance upwards, that the guards brought another to work in her place. Her hands were stiff and cold when she was made to give up the pick to the man beside her.

He was much bigger than the Captain, bigger than Talas or any of the Tlakwa men, and he was made to work blinded by a hood tied over his head. Guards passing behind him would pull on the thong tied around his neck, so he tried to work with it forward over his shoulder. He was also made to work naked, which Jenia saw made him take a great deal more care with his movements and efforts. It would make him easier for the guards to control. For all that he wouldn't get a rock chip in the eye because of the hood, he obviously missed his clothing more.

A guard struck her shoulder, and the pain of the blow cleared her head. Jenia realized she'd been wool-gathering there, lost in the bewildered feeling that came over her all too easily under Krummholz' gaze. Above the workers, on the rim of the quarry, the wizard could be seen, his grey robe outlined against the sky. He was watching them all. Jenia shuddered. From where she stood, it looked like he wore the Hunter Stars for a cloak, and the smaller moon on his shoulder like a love-knot, or a pet bird. He did not seem chilled, even under that open, starry sky, but his blue eyes were cold, shining in the moonlight. Not wanting those hard eyes to meet hers, Jenia looked down.

The guard drove her away from the pit hollowed into the limestone to where the baskets were being emptied into great smoking kilns. People threw basketfuls of broken limestone into an open kiln, and stoked the fire beneath another.

When that was opened, a broad-shouldered man was made to shovel out the baked lime. Waves of heat rose in the night air from the open kiln and from the heap of crumbling, baked lime. When it had cooled, he shovelled it into sacks like those her people made of hemp. These were held open by two very young men, hardly more than boys. At their age, perhaps eleven summers, they would not have been allowed to travel alone to a May festival at neighbouring villages among her people, but they would have wanted to. She took the next sack from their tired hands.

"I can do this," she said. "You rest." They understood what she meant, if not her words, and looked timidly at the guard. Clearly rest was not allowed. "Can they bring water, then?" she asked, for the heat from the kiln was fierce, and the bare shoulders of the man with the shovel were slick with sweat. "Water?" She mimed drinking from a cupped hand.

It earned her a cut from the guard's whip across her shoulder. The boys were careful not to look at her as they were sent with empty baskets to the quarry. The man beside her began shovelling lime so that she was hard-pressed to keep the sack open for filling. Eventually she tied it with twine, swung it aside with effort, and took an empty sack from a nearby heap. This work was enough like bagging potatoes in fall that her hands could work without conscious effort, and after a while her head began to clear.

"Nice try," said the man under his breath, and she looked up at him suddenly, over the open mouth of the sack that that was being filled.

It was Ronay, stripped to his sandals and a layer of sweat and lime dust. A piece of linen was tied across his lower face, and she hadn't recognized him at first.

Jenia looked to see if any guards were near, not by turning her head, but moving only her eyes. "I knew better," she muttered. "I should have remembered."

"Hard to think," he grunted.

There was a kerchief tucked inside Jenia's shirt, and she tied it across her own face, remembering how Tared had coughed till he bled. This lime wasn't like the lime gardeners used; it made her hands sting after a while. The rough hempen sacks seemed to wear her skin raw faster than she remembered from working with potato sacks. *Wherever this wizard is getting his sacks from,* she thought grimly, *they're doing a lousy job making them. Hemp doesn't have to be this rough. If he steals people for a night and a day, he must be stealing sacks, too.* It was an odd thought, that the sacks might have travelled farther than she had on her journey. Or perhaps the hemp had been grown, retted, spun and woven in a village just outside the quarry. There was no way she could know. And it didn't matter, so long as she had an open sack waiting when Ronay filled the shovel with lime.

They filled almost two dozen sacks together before that kiln was empty, and moved together to the next one. Ronay said nothing more to her, only kept the shovel moving smoothly, changing his grip from time to time. When there was a pause before one or another kiln was opened, he would set down the shovel and stretch, but if he tried to sit or lay on the hard ground the guards would kick him with their hard boots. Jenia found more of the rough sacks and kept armfuls of them with her. She did not want to appear idle, and be made to work elsewhere in the quarry.

It was daylight before Ronay noticed as Jenia bent to pick up each sack, she put a hand under her brown woollen shirt now smeared with lime dust. His glance seemed to ask a question he could not speak aloud, for there was a guard at that moment supervising the opening of a kiln. By noon, as they were both staggering with weariness, Ronay had finally seen what Jenia held in one small fist as she opened the sacks for him to fill, and what she was hiding in the middle of the lime in each sack. She knew he saw, and she watched as he filled the shovel again, then moving carefully emptied it once, twice and again into the next sack she held open.

If he drew any attention to what she was doing, the guards would notice. Jenia was too tired for careful sleight-of-hand, and was hoping no one else would see. She tied the sack, set it aside, and reached for one more. When this one was filled, the kiln was empty of baked lime. Ronay stood aside as a guard began driving a line of people forward to empty baskets of broken rock into the kiln.

Either the guards were tired also, though they at least were given water and a chance to sit while on duty, or they did not think to watch her closely. They had not thought to search her, after all, and had no more curiosity about the thickness of her waist than the beggar-woman and the noble she had seen walk past, lugging a basket of crushed limestone between their swollen bellies.

There was no water given to the workers. The kerchief across Jenia's face was caked with white dust that crumbled when she brushed it away. Never had she known such thirst, not even when standing dizzy in grain fields with Tared's scythe in her hands. The lime burned in raw places on her wrists and arms. Her calloused hands kept busy, dry and hard on the rough sacks but still deftly tying the lengths of twine.

She was well enough, compared to others working under the hot sun. Heat broiled down on them all out of an achingly blue sky, a foreign sky to Jenia after Copper Island's shafts of sunlight breaking through cool grey clouds. Sweat no longer gleamed on Ronay's sunburned back, but his hands were damp on the shovel handle as blisters rose and broke. She saw two men steal mouthfuls of water from a discoloured puddle behind the kilns. They died later that afternoon, with cracked and bleeding mouths. They weren't the boys whom she replaced at holding the sacks — she thought not, but she could not tell one shuffling, dusty figure from another by then.

Once she thought she saw Tared, stirring lime and broken rocks together, and she almost cried out. But it was Ronay turning from the kiln with his shovel filled, and she shut her mouth around whatever words might have come, and held the waiting sack open between her cracked hands. Another time Dela was staggering past with a half-full basket, but it was the beggar-woman she had seen earlier, now wearing the noble's scarf like a sling tied under the swell of her belly.

Sunset was colouring the sky before the workers were made at last to gather in a group near the heap of tied sacks. Jenia was awed to see how many she had tied with her own hands, working all day and most of the night. She'd never sacked that many potatoes at harvest. Even her village's bins of apples for cider-making had never been stacked so high. Suddenly she missed the taste of apples, and the thought of biting into one with a crunch and tasting the sweet juice made her mouth water. She licked her dry lips. *I miss my apple trees,* she thought, and pressed her hands against the growl of hunger in her empty stomach. The bag tied against her waist was empty now under her loose shirt, and even her earrings had gone into the last two sacks.

"I thought you wanted to work with me," Ronay said almost inaudibly under his breath as he stood behind her. Jenia didn't turn, and the workers beside her either didn't hear him speak or were too numbed by exhaustion to react. "I thought you wanted to be near me, for me to protect you from the guards. I thought maybe you cared to be close to me. Then I saw. Nice bit of work, that. What will those nails do?"

She didn't trust her voice to be quiet enough to go unheard. She looked down, past her dusty clothes and the bare legs of the woman next to her. "Do you play dice? Or throw stones? I wouldn't want to bet against you." Ronay's breath stirred her hair as his blood dripped quietly from the tips of his cramped fingers. She watched the drops fall on her boots, speckling the scuffed leather. "Curse me, you've worked me till I'm past weeping and beyond pain...but I wouldn't stop while a slip of a girl could still keep up. And then when I saw, I wouldn't leave a fighter alone on the field."

Jenia didn't breathe. Keeping her head down, she glanced around, trying not to be seen looking around. There! On the edge of the quarry, Krummholz was raising his hands. The mound of sacks faded from sight, and the wizard's face showed satisfaction.

Relief and triumph surged in her breast, but Jenia fought to make no outward sign. *If he doesn't notice me for a few more moments...* Rigid with fear and suppressed elation, Jenia waited for what seemed an eternity until Krummholz summoned his energies again and the dust-caked workers began to fade from sight. One dusty figure slumped in death, even as he faded, and another fell to her knees. Some workers opened cracked lips to cry out in fear or bewilderment, but the expression on Ronay's face was curiosity — and his gaze was fixed on Jenia as first one leg, then the other gave way at last and she began to fall, turning as she went. "There is a place for you here," he was saying softly, and he laid his bleeding hand over his heart as he faded from her sight.

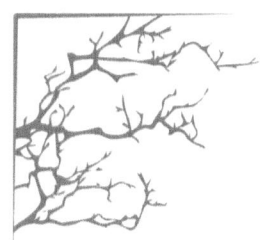

Chapter Eleven

J enia kept turning as she fell onto the sand, smooth and ribbed-hard by the
tide that had come in and gone out again and again. A gull wheeled
overhead, screeching through mist, and a child screeched too. She rolled, lying
on damp sand, to see young Lop with a basket spilled underfoot. A small white
dog shied away from Jenia and barked.

"Tsusiat!" the child wailed, then turned and ran through the mist, calling
again. "Tsusiat! She fell out of the air. Tsusiat! She just fell!" Small feet pounded
over the storm-tossed logs, and Lop disappeared in the direction of the Tlakwa
houses. The dog retreated, still barking, and ran after the child.

Following slowly, Jenia pulled the dusty kerchief from her face. She needed
water so badly, it was hard to think.

But once I drink and wash, I know what to do. Her dry lips cracked as she
smiled. *I know what to tell them all.* The mist was a cool blessing on her face and
hands, but the dust began to sting in her cuts.

Tsusiat was shocked to see her dusty and red-eyed after a cloudy day. "I
thought you were resting and learning more herbs with Karn," was all Tsusiat
could say. They walked together to the small creek, not upstream to the
women's quiet bathing place, but near the houses so that Jenia could quickly
drink and wash. The dust had sifted through her clothes to her skin, and itched.

While Jenia soaked her sweat- and dust-stained clothes, Tsusiat sent Lop
to borrow something for Jenia to wear. "You'll be cold when you come out,"
Tsusiat said from the bank above the clay creek bed, and stripped to enter the
water and wash the dust from Jenia's rough hair. "What happened today? Did
the magic come for you again? It must have. There's the mark of a whip, and
your forehead is sunburned."

But Jenia said nothing about her sudden reappearance on the beach until
later. That tale was for telling indoors, by the fire, when she was clean with a
blanket wrapped around the fresh bruises and whip cuts. With a bowl of soup

in her hand, if she could get it. When she first came here, she'd had to sing for her supper, as her mother would say, and tell her story well enough to make it clear she was a welcome guest at their fire. Now the villagers were impatient to hear her what she had to say. What Ronay would tell his waiting soldiers, well, that was his own telling to do. But it mattered to her what the Tlakwa people thought of her news.

She got all she asked for — the steaming bowl, the place by the fire, and Tsusiat's own blanket around her shoulders. Two children went running to the soldier's tents with a bowl of Karn's salve and fresh mendwell for Ronay, at her request. That showed how well these people regarded her. But even so, when she told her tale, she could not call them to rise up and take arms against the wizard in his half-built tower.

They would not fight. They would not even argue.

"Krummholz is not all-powerful and all-knowing," Jenia said proudly. "With careful planning, he can be resisted and his plans confounded. We must work together to bring him down."

"We must?" Talas picked up a half-finished carving, turning it over in his hands. He sat on a floor mat, with a lamp on a wooden bin at his elbow.

"Leaving an evil man to do wicked deeds is the same as doing that wickedness ourselves," Jenia insisted. She put the steaming bowl of soup down on a bench, away from the fur of some great cat, a fur eerily like the pelt of the cat-snake she had seen in the bogs.

Talas pulled a mat over his lap to catch chips, and began whittling away at the wood with a carving knife. "Is it?"

Is he only the spokesman for these people? I thought he would be their defender, too. Jenia tried again. "It is our duty not to leave him unharried when we have the ability to resist him."

"Why?" He met her angry glare for a moment, then returned to his carving. No one else would even speak to her, but busied themselves with sewing, or mending tools and other tasks. They were still within earshot near the great hearth, just carefully out of the conversation.

"We must do what we can to bring him down," Jenia said to the people who had fed her and sheltered her, and were still making her welcome at their hearth. "You're not saying that we ought to leave him to continue using people up and throwing them away?"

"We're not saying that," Talas answered mildly. "We have done what we can. We are not fighters except in small bands. We fight where we must, and only to protect."

"Well, this would be to protect yourselves," Jenia pointed out. "Do you want to have a wizard for your neighbour if this is how he uses his powers? What about when he takes one of your own?"

"We protect ourselves in other ways, and fight only when we must." His callused thumb brushed against the animal face becoming clearer in the wood, one with big blunt teeth like chisels. "We can do nothing in a battle against a wizard. He cannot be brought down by force of arms. It takes a wizard to know what will control another wizard."

"If we do not take up arms and resist him, we'll be doing no more than…" Jenia groped for words.

"Than you did when you and your brother and sister laboured there?" Tsusiat said softly, across the fire. "When you were beaten with whips for learning the shapes of the mountains, and the trees, so you would know this place truly after walking every step of the distance you had been first brought to by magic?"

Jenia's anger flared at Tsusiat now. "If we don't stand up and show that he can't do these cruel things without facing the consequences, we'll be as passive as his workers are under his spell."

"As you were when you left pieces of clay among the gravel, and taught your fellows to do the same?" In the firelight, Tsusiat's brown eyes were black, unreadable. "You said that in your village you make your homes in wattle-and-daub. Clay soaked in water swells, as you know. Your hands must have known it, even bewildered by magic. I would not like to guess what happens to dry clay when mixed into that gravel porridge you described — but I think that by chance you will have weakened the materials of which the tower is being made."

"It was not by chance! It was not only by using clay that I tried to resist him," Jenia said then, fighting down her pride in order to keep a firm grip on her storytelling. She was having a much harder time than she had expected, but she kept trying to win the Tlakwa people to fight with her. "I brought my bag of iron nails with me, tied under my clothing, when I was taken by magic for the third time. At the quarry, when I held the sacks to be filled with lime from the kilns, I put a nail into each sack. Even my earrings, rusting as they were, were hidden in the lime."

Talas blew shavings from his carving. "And what will that do?"

The rain was beating steadily down upon the roof overhead, and gusts of wind brought cold drops in through the smoke hole. "In this weather, they were already rusted," she said wryly. "In that porridge of stone and lime, they could only be pockets of corruption, not strong bars like the posts and lintels of a house."

"If such a one as you, who claim to have no magic, can find this way to resist the wizard and confound his plans, then he will surely fall before the strength of mighty wizards from the south." Talas stretched out his legs, resting both feet on a block of wood waiting next to the fire.

"What do you mean, I claim to have no magic?" Jenia snapped. "I haven't so much as an old hedge-witch's chants and simples. And there is no sign of these other wizards." She bit her lip. *Sometimes I think I understand even Krummholz better than these people. I know I understand him better than Ronay or his lord. Krummholz uses people up and moves them around like a threshing crew but across great distances, not across a valley. Ronay and his lord think people should agree when they're told where to go and when to stay. I miss my apple trees.*

"Karn took you in to live in her house," said Tsusiat softly. "Did she sing you a tune that wanders on and on, repeating itself?" At Jenia's sullen nod, Tsusiat smiled. "That one names all the herbs growing in her garden. And I can see that you have no new stings and bites on your arms or anywhere — have the insects begun to leave you alone, as they do Karn?"

Stunned, Jenia looked at her own hands. She couldn't remember when she had last slapped one of the annoying, whining insects. "There aren't any of them, here in your houses..."

"The wood smoke keeps them out, but we are still followed when outdoors. Karn is never bitten or stung, even when she used to walk inland near the bogs. She used to do that, no matter how forbidden it is to the rest of us, right up until her bones were too stiff late this spring. I think she sings something every few days, and it keeps the insects away, but it never works for me." Tsusiat's good-humoured chuckle warmed Jenia's stiff mood. "Of course I tried it! I can remember anything I hear even once, if I pay attention, and Karn knows that. I think she knew it wouldn't work for me. And she expected it to work for you, for all that she said you are no great wizard."

"If I were a great wizard, I'd understand what I've been seeing and doing under Krummholz's spells." Jenia slumped down onto a bench across the fire from where Tsusiat sat with small feet neatly together. "Why didn't he build a tower from wood, like your houses? Or quarry out blocks of stone from the mountains here, instead of carrying a hundred thousand bushel basketfuls of gravel from some distant prairie?"

"Maybe he didn't want to take anything away from the mountains." Tsusiat pushed two of the burning chunks of wood closer together in the fire pit. "Maybe the point was bringing something from far away to the Island. For magical reasons. To build his Tower."

Jenia shivered. She reached for her bowl, but the soup had gone cold. "I can't understand that reasoning. I can only remember how sharp the stones were, and how the lime burned in my cuts and blisters."

"Do you think Krummholz remembers that?"

"No."

"Then you know something he does not. You know something of how pain, even from little hurts, can distract you from thinking and reasoning clearly. And so can his magic."

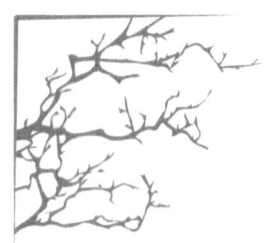

Chapter Twelve

Something woke her. It was Talas, calling out from the beach near Karn's home. Jenia rose from her pallet, rubbing sleep from her eyes, and pulled on some clothes — anything, the first things that came to hand. Glancing over at Karn's bed, she saw the old woman's eyes glitter before slitting shut, as Karn lay still without rising. Let her pretend to be asleep, so that Jenia would see what the noise was about and light the morning fire. It didn't bother her enough to matter, not when Talas was calling again, with a note of urgency in his voice. She stumbled out the door, almost running into him at the weather-silvered bench where Karn would sit in the afternoon sun. The sand was cold under her bare feet, but Talas' bare chest was beaded with sweat from his run.

"Tsusiat is gone," he said.

She didn't know what he meant at first, then realization dawned.

"No footprints, no signs. The blankets still show the outline of a body where Tsusiat lay down to sleep at sunset last night." The scent of wood smoke hung around him in the clear morning air, even after his run.

"If you'd listened to me—"

"We were not wrong," said Talas, and Jenia knew it was so. "No one sets out to fight a raid or a battle at night in the rain, not by choice. We set out and did our part to fight this battle many days ago, when you came to us."

"What? What did you do?" she said bitterly. "What could a village of singers and berry-pickers possibly have done? None of you could stand against a wizard whose magic brings strong fighters quaking to their knees. Krummholz has armoured guards to kill the few not frozen with fear. You gave me shelter, that was all you could do."

"We sent word with our traders to the cities in the South. Wizards always hear the news. Where do you think Tsusiat was for those days, but singing your story to the Tellers at Opitsat?" Talas asked without rancour. "The story went south with many boats, and is still being told. Wizards will hear of this upstart here in the Tlakwa wilderness, and they will know what to do with him."

"And that's enough?" She would never understand these people's reasoning, never in a thousand years, not even if Tsusiat told her a story and sang her a song for each and every reason they made a decision.

"It seems enough." Talas hesitated. "It was surely enough until I woke this morning, and no one knew where or how Tsusiat was gone from our house. It would be enough, if I could know that Tsusiat will return as you did, beaten and sore each time, but well enough even after hard treatment."

In horror, Jenia felt her hands grow cold and her legs tremble. Her own brother and sister were not the only ones who suffered more than she did under the magic. She saw again slack-jawed faces and dull eyes of people who slumped, bruised and imbecilic, against the quarry walls. She remembered the people falling dead as she faded away from the gravel pit, back to the beach with a dead woman's blood drying on her hands. And for those whose pride or strength overcame the spells of fear and bewilderment, there were the cruel guards, and nothing more to hope for than the cliff and wave-swept stones far below.

Talas saw her sure knowledge that Tsusiat was in grave danger. "I cannot take our fighters to raid a man who can kill them with a word and a wave of his arm," he said desperately. "To find men who love war enough to face a wizard, I would have to go farther than Opitsat. The soldiers have left their camp."

"When?"

"This morning as I began to run here. They left tents, packs, everything but their weapons. They were marching inland, ready to fight." Talas shuddered. "I cannot wait here to see if any of them come back alive."

"I cannot wait here to see what will be found in Tsusiat's bed tonight," Jenia said with as much despair. "I cannot wait here to be taken again."

She whirled and ran back inside, to the small pile of her clothing and pack. Hands shaking, Jenia forced herself to dress properly and completely from the skin out. Talas came to stand in the doorway as she fastened her belt and pulled her boots on, and began rummaging through her pack.

Linens. Whetstone. Mending kit. Wooden bowl. Spice bundle. Salt. None of this or anything else in it would be of any use. She threw the pack against the wall, then snatched it up again.

"What are you doing?" Karn asked from her bed in the far corner.

"Looking for my pruning knife."

"You think that will arm you against a true wizard?" Karn didn't even lift her head from the pillow. "Wizards can protect themselves from weapons, heal injuries—"

"I'm not going through that poisoned bog again without it."

Jenia found her knife in its sheath and slipped it onto her belt, buckling it again as she looked at the morning sky, past Talas who stood silently in the doorway.

The day was already bright and clear. Jenia would not need her cloak for warmth; but then she thought of the cat-snake and the venom it spat. Perhaps the cloak would keep another beast's venom from spraying onto her skin. Jenia fastened her cloak with trembling hands, thinking with one absurdly clear part of her mind about how she had never been hunted by any of the afflicted beasts when she was inland alone, while Ronay's soldiers and the Tlakwa villagers saw them if they went further than the shoreline meadows and forests.

"You are going to the tower," Talas said, and it took her a moment to hear him and nod in response. "Then you do know where it is."

"Yes. I saw it. It's being built on the shoulder of a mountain above a beach with a whale carcass, long-dead." Jenia tried to think where she walked in her search. "That may be the beach Tsusiat calls Please-be-bones. There's a poisoned bog on the inland shoulder of the mountain, where water is being drawn to make that stone porridge."

"There will be creatures," he warned her.

"They only bothered me once I was found by the soldiers." Jenia wondered why that was so. And then she knew. "They won't bother me at all — they didn't the first night I slept outdoors on the island. They track people by scent, like the smoke in your hair and clothes, and the sweat in the felt lining of the soldiers' armour. Karn is never troubled by the beasts because of her bathing ritual. She made me air my clothes yesterday and bathe last night. I'll be fine," she said with more confidence than she felt.

"We cannot come inland with you, on the forbidden ground, for your hopeless attack," he said, looking away.

"I didn't expect that," she said tightly. "But you could take your boats around the headlands to that beach, to see if it is the right one. I couldn't see any easy way from the shore up to where the tower is being built, but you should be able to see it from your boats. You might even see him order his guards to throw me off the cliff. That would make another fine song for you to send south with your Traders."

"What if Tsusiat has been stolen to another place, not to work at the tower?" he asked suddenly. "What will you do then?"

The thought made her go weak at the knees. Jenia had no idea how far away the prairie with the gravel pit or the plains with the lime quarry were. If Tsusiat were at either of those places, there was nothing to do but wait for the magic return at sunset. "Then I'll...trim a hedge around his empty tower," she said lamely.

"And if the wizard is there, with Tsusiat and other people trapped by his magic?" Talas moved away from the doorway, to let her go out. "What will you do?"

"Whatever I do will be more than you do, which is nothing," she added bitterly. It wasn't fair! Talas was strong enough for travel, and adventures, and fighting. He knew Copper Island far better than she could in a few weeks. Why should she be the one setting out for battle, with a pruning knife on her belt and her narrow boots shaking on Karn's hard-packed floor?

"I came to tell you, didn't I?"

She couldn't tell what he was thinking. "And you'll bring the boats round where I'm going?"

"I can do that," he said, expressionless. "If you wish."

She pushed through the doorway past him, leaving behind the scent of wood smoke and sweat drying on his chest.

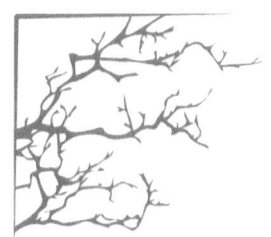

Chapter Thirteen

J enia stood at the edge of the scrubby pine grove, where a few shards of gravel ground under her boots into the mossy turf.

There were no puddles here, no dampness underfoot. Had it not rained here lately? The Tlakwa village had been under a cloudburst last night, on the same island and under the same weather, but here the ground and twisted trees showed no sign of last night's torrential rain. This must be another work of magic by Krummholz. *Good, then,* Jenia decided. *Another way for him to spend his energies. If he sends the stones or the lime to its destination first, and then returns the workers, he isn't able to do everything at once.* Jenia hoped a downpour would strike at any minute, to divide the wizard's attention at a crucial moment, but that seemed about as likely as a thunderbolt from the clear blue sky.

She sighed. *Ah, we can't have everything we want, or we'd all stay by the fire.* Time to work her way closer, if possible, to search for Tsusiat and for the high point where she had spotted Krummholz.

She hid herself against the great bole of a hemlock that twisted up out of the peat like a bone pitchfork. Even in the seasoned, dry wood under her hands she could feel the illness in this tree and the trees around her. There was no longer any abundance in this soil for these trees; they were gasping and grasping for earth and water that would sustain them. The trees felt like flesh swollen in boils and infection. She felt they cried out for lancing and searing, to be cleansed with blade and fire.

It hardened her heart to learn Krummholz harmed more lives than just the humans he stole to do his labour. She undid her heavy cloak and let it fall. She then took a firm grip on her pruning knife and scratched into the weather-silvered wood of the hemlock a T for Tared, a D for Dela and between those letters, an O for the lost babe. *Now this wood knows my knife,* she thought. *Now it is mine, like the apple boughs I grafted at home and the plum tree in Kultis that dropped its wasp nest and helped me. Now its twisted strength is in me.* Then she passed round the tree and edged closer to the work site.

None of the workers passing on the narrow gravel road a stone's throw away saw her, burdened as they were with pails of bog-water. Others ferried pails of gravel and sacks of lime to troughs to be mixed. With a start Jenia realized she was actually closer by far to Krummholz than she ever was when called by magic to his work sites.

It was like the time Tared had struck an anthill hidden in a barley field, and with one blow of his scythe had sheared off the top. *There must be two hundred people, milling everywhere like ants trooping in lines. How can even a dozen guards be enough to keep them in order?* Shaking her head to clear her thoughts, Jenia forced the memory away, as a billowing white cloud blew up from the south. She saw some broad, rough hands and faces burned brown as Tlakwa faces, on people paler than herself where they usually wore clothing. Other hands were slim and delicate, and it took two pairs of those hands to carry a single basket of stones. She couldn't bear to look at the faces of any of these people. *Only look at their hands, cut and blistered.* The clothes of the workers were a bewildering variety of loose shirts for sleeping, linen loincloths, and embroidered finery dyed saffron-bright or an unfamiliar blue she had never seen before, and all of it smudged with lime dust and peat-stained water, fluttering in a breeze gone suddenly cool. There were men of all sizes, stumbling, with hoods on the largest and those who seemed most alert. There were women of every age, from slim maidens to stocky grandmothers; and against a foundation wall in one corner, a woman struggled, panting hard, swollen belly rippling under her linen. There was gravel spilled over her feet from a dropped basket. A shadow passed over the labouring woman as a cloud drifted over the sun.

Forcing her horrified gaze away, Jenia looked into the scrubby forest edging the clearing. A small movement caught her attention, some dozens of yards away and close to the ledge that must be above the stony beach. It was Ronay's bronze helmet she saw, a dull gleam under the grey clouds boiling up out of the southern sky. Hiding behind the broad bole of a fallen tree, he was almost invisible. *I never expected he would come here. He moved to let me see him,* she knew suddenly, when he looked over at her and back to the guards who patrolled with all their attention on the workers. *His soldiers must be there, too.*

Ready to strike. Almost time. Can they feel it too? Something is coming, said her hand on a scabbed pine tree and her feet on the damp ground, with her cropped hair rising to stand on end. *Something big. Something awful.*

It was then she saw Tsusiat, straining to carry two pails of the peat-stained bog-water. Tsusiat never needed Talas' broad shoulders or his great strength to be able to work until others gave up in exhaustion, but the corded muscles in those brown arms were trembling. *Is that mud or blood staining Tsusiat's bare feet?* Jenia couldn't tell. *I have to know. Now. No more waiting. Now.*

She stepped forward from the dubious cover of the crooked, scrubby pines, and took a deep breath of air gone thin, with the scents of salt ocean and dusty sage. With that first step several things happened almost in the same moment.

Jenia realized from this slight distance, and with the thoughts that had led her to draw her pruning knife without knowing it, she would soon be noticed by the guards or certainly by the wizard himself. At that moment, Tsusiat's gaze swung upward, though the dark head and tanned face was lowered. Jenia burned in an agony of sympathy for how quickly the manners of a slave and a drudge were learned. Tsusiat and Jenia saw each other across some fifty yards of open space, past the wizard who stood between them.

Tsusiat always understands me. A word, a glance.... Tsusiat always understands what I mean. In a heartbeat Jenia knew the wizard must be noticing Tsusiat's expression change. He would be turning to see what lay behind him, where Tsusiat was looking. She pointed with one hand at the spring casing beside her friend, who instantly understood. Without hesitation, Tsusiat emptied both stinking pails of bogwater into the clean basin of the spring. The casing rang like a bell, and cracked.

It was enough. Krummholz started at the noise, and turned to see what had happened to the spring. Lightning struck then out of the billowing clouds, in blows quick as a woodpecker tapping, startling everyone: first the highest point of the unfinished tower, then the second stroke angled lower to strike the base. Screaming, scores of the workers dropped their burdens and scattered, while others stood flat-footed and staring. *Lightning doesn't do that,* Jenia knew, and she smiled to see the wizard gather his wits. As Krummholz made a warding gesture, the third stroke skidded away from him, driving a score of the workers burnt and bleeding into the bog. Jenia met Ronay's gaze and moved her left hand as she'd seen the Captain do, fighting the cat-snake, when he sent his woman soldier Marta ahead and to one side.

Without hesitation, Ronay led his seven soldiers out of cover. Two guards were down and bleeding before he'd taken a dozen strides. At the sound of the soldiers' boots on gravel, Krummholz spun with his grey robes still swirling the other way, to see what was happening where steel swords struck at bronze armour. The wizard's hands rose, and he flung handfuls of empty air toward the struggle. All the soldiers and guards alike were bowled over, mowing down lines of dull-eyed workers like wheat at harvest. One guard burst, a bag of blood against the foundation of the tower, his helmet and sword flying to strike down two workers. Their screams cut off in choking gasps. When the next bolt of lightning streaked toward him, Krummholz fended it away and into a group of workers cowering together. *Wasn't Tsusiat among them?* Jenia's heart was in her mouth. *They're burnt and shattered....*

Hatred gave Jenia speed to run forward, closer than she dared to the wizard, who still had not seen her. *Twisted, unnatural beast, no peace for you,* she cursed him with words she had learned from Karn and from Ronay, and from the cold wind that blew in with the lightning. *Let bronze and steel lay you open, spilling your blood like winter rain. Let the lightning strike you down.* It felt like when she had darted forward to prick at a coil of the cat-snake, between the poisoned fangs and the sharp tail. She didn't know she had the daring to keep her hands steady, as she held her bronze knife high by her cheek, feeling the balanced blade as she threw it. The edge whistled, cutting the air. She knew that sound, from Ronay's steel sword passing near her face in the bog. *My blade is that swift,* she thought. *My blade strikes home.* Sparkling in a shaft of sunlight, her knife spun as it flew, guided by all the skill in her small hand. Her knife struck the wizard squarely between the shoulder blades, passed in for half its length, and as she watched, unable to breathe for shock at what she had done, it quivered. *If armies are mostly a distraction from the real battle,* she knew, *I've surely distracted him now.*

The knife slipped out of his back and fell underfoot as he turned, swiftly now, and saw her. All the hair rose, all over her body. *He knows me!* Her heart failed. Lightning struck the tower behind him, and into the fleeing workers, scattering them bleeding into the bog, but neither the wizard nor Jenia even flinched. *I've never met his gaze before, but he knows everything about me,* and her heart knew it was true. A dark cloud boiled out of the clear sky over the wizard's head. In the wizard's eyes, Jenia saw his fury gather. She stumbled backwards, five yards, ten, and another few feet before her knees turned to water and her hands balled into useless fists, and when the shadow of his cloud fell over her, her cropped hair stood out in fear. *No peace for you.*

It didn't appear to be his cloud after all, for the lightning that issued from it streaked down to strike him, not Jenia. The next bolt shattered the spring basin, and a third set the bog to boiling behind her as she fell to the ground, cowering and deafened by thunder. *Laughing? What old woman is laughing? Her laughter echoes all around, cheering on the stronger wrestler in a contest, praising the fastest runner in a race, and jeering at the loser. It's echoing off the trees behind me to the slumped mountain and back, and it's pulling me to my feet.*

She gasped for breath. Branches of twisted pine trees fell around her, and Jenia covered her head with her hands. Dank, foul steam from the bog spilled over the site of the tower, and half-seen through that fog ran the panicking workers. Pails of stones and bog-water spilled, forgotten underfoot when the workers woke from their misery. There was no shelter for guards or workers even in the half-built tower.

No shelter, for the next time the lightning struck, it cracked the stony walls and with it came rain out of the boiling grey clouds. Water pounded out of the sky like waves on a shore, in gusts that beat Jenia down each time she tried to see what was happening. Tumbling past her came rags of clothing and tree branches, and someone's shattered arm caught in the wind.

When she was able to raise her head, she saw the half-built tower melting like a sand village. Cracks opened in the stone walls and split apart the pavement underfoot, but fear gave some workers speed to run for the forest. Great swollen clay-streaks and stains of rust showed where the walls crumbled and broke under the pounding rain.

It was like watching the weathering of ten years' rain all at once on an abandoned cottage of wattle and daub, and suddenly that was how Jenia saw the ruin of the tower. It was no longer a mighty stronghold to be brought down by force of arms. Now the stony, stained heap seemed no greater than the knee-high mound of beach sand Lop had shaped for a day, defended by useless dikes against the rising tide, and which had collapsed under the boots of Ronay's soldiers when they arrived at the village's home beach.

Still Jenia did not shout or cheer, for her mouth and eyes were filled with the driving rain, and the stink of the lightning bolts was in her lungs. Her ears rang, and popped as she swallowed the sour wind. Lightning struck the ruin again, and into the bog behind her.

Then another stink hung about her, a rank animal smell. Before she could turn her head to see what had come out of the rain or the bog, a strong arm was braced on the ground by her head. Ronay was crouched over her, helmet dented and his armour splattered with blood. He cursed as a spray of gravel rattled against his armour.

Then he was on his feet, pulling her up. "Move!" he shouted. They scrambled some yards away through the pounding rain, Jenia not knowing why until the top of a dead-white tree crashed to the ground where she had been crouched. She stared; it was driven into the gravel like a pitchfork into hay.

"I saw you tell your friend what to do," Ronay shouted at her ear. "Good timing, Sergeant. You still give good orders." The wind ebbed to more ordinary gusts, and the rain subsided till it was falling in a steady curtain over the wreckage of the worksite. The stench of burnt flesh swept over Jenia in one gust, and as the wind wheeled about the next gust carried a fog of boiling blood in the bog. Her stomach heaving, Jenia fell to her knees and vomited, twice and a third time, guts clenching though there was nothing to bring up but bile. She felt Ronay's hard hand squeeze her shoulder for an instant. "Those guards are coming to their senses. They'll be rallying soon. I'd better put a stop to that."

And he set out to do precisely that, directing his few soldiers on unfamiliar ground. The guards were more bewildered than the workers, if anything, but despair did not lessen their ferocity. It was more frightening than nameless lightning bolts, to see the work of swords on flesh. *It's worse than the cat-snake, it's ugly...* Jenia shuddered and turned away, looking for Tsusiat. *There are so many bodies!* She stumbled past awful things, teeth and hands tangled in pine *boughs and tattered rags. That man is whole, but for his head twisted round...there are so many dead! And I had wanted the Tlakwa to fight. I had no idea, no real idea what a battle is like, not even after being beaten or facing the cat-snake.*

She made a wide circle around the blackened body of the wizard and came upon the broken casing of the spring, but it was Tsusiat who found her kneeling there, as the rain stopped. The water was still flowing out of the rock, and draining out of the cracked basin. As the spring water welled up, the foul bog-water drained away and the basin was washed clean. Jenia dipped her hands to cup the clear water, and raised it into a shaft of sunlight as the clouds parted. The last gusts of wind tore sparkling drops from her hands to patter like raindrops on Tsusiat's bare legs and arms, beside her.

"The water is clean again," said Tsusiat, and drank from Jenia's cupped hands.

Relief washed over Jenia, and through her. She had swum in the surf with Tsusiat after butchering the whale, and had thought then that she knew what it was like to wash clean. Now the returning sunlight warmed her soaked clothing, a comfort she had not looked for.

Jenia's hand fell against one of the pails Tsusiat had dropped. It was broken, but the other pail was whole. Fumbling, Jenia rinsed it out, rubbing the inside with her calloused hand, and set the pail to catch the overflow from the spring. *Others will be thirsty,* she knew. "There's a woman who was giving birth," she said. "We should find her, and—"

"She is dead," said Tsusiat. "There were trees falling and the wall collapsed. She could not run. At least she is buried. There are so many dead, and we cannot learn any of their names and take them to the funeral islet off-shore. We will have to bury them here, without names." Tsusiat stood carefully, favouring tired muscles, and walked a few steps to look out from the cliff. "The boats are coming into the bay," Tsusiat said. "Look, our own boats, and my good brother with his steering paddle in his best boat. I can bring some of these people down the cliff. Can you bring the rest around to the village by the way you took?"

Startled, Jenia saw behind Tsusiat that Ronay was with his prisoners, disarmed and bound. The clouds wisped away overhead, burning off in the bright day's returning sunlight. Jenia got to her feet, a little unsteady on the wet ground, and made her way past fluttering scraps of linen and someone's burnt foot, still in its sandal, to the dead tree that had been driven into the gravel path. With magic, Krummholz had brought people and gravel to build this place. With magic, he stole strength from the bog-water and stone, leaving the trees twisted with limbs contorted like people in pain.

Now Jenia could feel the spring flowing clean, and the gravel path slippery underfoot, but not treacherous. Now she could feel the trees, even without touching them, the day's new growth as healthy and straight as it knew how to lay itself. Always, the old growth would remain twisted, but in the bog-water lapping her boots at the edge of the path, Jenia felt no more taint. It was only bog-water, sour and stained with peat and blood. No longer was the strength of this place being sapped from the trees and water, tapped by the wizard for his own purposes. She felt the strength in a thicket of trees, bent by the offshore wind and springing upwards still for its own reasons.

She put both her small hands to one of the spires of the dead tree skewered into the gravel, and pulled. It split away, as if the lightning had parted it for her. The grain of the limb had twisted completely around on itself three times, in a span longer than she was tall. She held it like a spear, or a scythe or a walking stick. "Let's do what we can, together," she said.

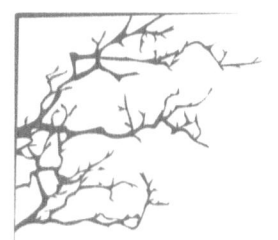

Chapter Fourteen

Smoke was rising from the smoke holes of the great houses in the Tlakwa village when the boats rounded the headland. Jenia watched the best pullers in the village bring home their boats, overloaded with weary and battered strangers. As she led the way along the shoreline path from Karn's empty house, those who had not descended the cliff with Tsusiat followed behind her, footsore and weary. Ronay and his soldiers brought up the rear with the former guards who had been made prisoners.

The fresh offshore breeze blew the last of the confusion out of all their minds. The narrow boats were being pulled high up on their home beach as Jenia led her battered crowd toward the steam for bathing, and the village fires with the scents of broiled meat and soups rich with meat and herbs.

There was a bowl or a cup for everyone, and a warm shawl or blanket, and more food cooking in great wooden boxes of water heated with stones from the fires. "After the thunder, Karn told us to prepare a feast for a hundred visitors and more," said Lema, putting a bowl into Jenia's hands. "And to bring out every blanket we owned."

Jenia drank down the hot broth in one long gulp before shrugging out of her wet clothes and boots in Tsusiat's alcove. Tsusiat's blanket was big enough to wrap around herself twice, and it held the scent of her friend, wood smoke and clean hair and minty herb tea. Leaving her twisted branch leaning against the wall, she went to find a place near the fire, where Karn sat, nodding, huddled inside her new shawl.

Her grey head bobbed up for a moment, and Karn blinked weary eyes. "It's growing dark," she said. "Bring out the lamps." Then she spoke a word, one Jenia could never remember clearly afterwards, and every lamp in all the alcoves of the great house flared into flame. Everyone was startled, but only the visitors were surprised. The villagers seemed reassured and continued with their duties, stepping quietly around Karn where she nodded off to sleep again on her bench.

Something touched Jenia's bare foot, and she looked down. It was young Lop, wrapping her feet in a rabbit fur. "You had an adventure. Will you tell me about it, one day under the two moons and the bright sun?" He waited for her promise before darting off out of sight. But not out of earshot, she knew.

Tsusiat slumped against her on the bench, clean now and in clean trousers and a patterned shawl, and weary to the bone, saying, "I'm cold." They leaned back-to-back on the bench, and gradually the warmth of the house and fire seeped into them. Lema took away their bowls and brought them back filled again with meat and boiled roots of a thin kind Jenia had never seen.

"Talas carried Karn to the village when he came back from her house," said Lema. "She lay down in Tsusiat's bed and went to sleep. After the thunder she got up and told us to start cooking."

"Was that all she said?" Tsusiat asked, still chewing.

Karn stirred on her bench. "I kept my vision to tell you, singer and storyteller." She opened her eyes, black in the firelight, and showed her teeth in a smile that made Jenia think of her own mother, after harvest, shutting the door on a full granary. "I rose out the smoke hole in my dream, and the wind blew a great bird up from the south. It was a bird I could see only in the shape of a cloud, and the curl of a wave. I rode with it, like a small dim bird clinging to its brightness. We spoke no words as we flew. I do not think the great bird even knew I was there.

"We flew together over the headlands and the low mountains of the island to a place twisted like the scar of a canker," said Karn, and her voice shook. "It was a bad place, swollen like a boil. There was something bright there I could only see in the crooked branches of the trees, and the broken stone trapped in mud. There was something dim standing straight and small there, like a knife before a spear.

"It took all of us, me, and the little dim one and the great one, to strike the crooked one at the centre of the twisted scar. No peace for him. We spilled his blood like winter rain. No trapped stones. We set them free. No poisoned bog to twist animals and trees. It is clean now of magic, and the blood and bone will rot into the peat." Karn's voice went thin as twisted thread. "The great one went away without looking back and I had to find my own way home." She got to her feet, wobbling, and Lema put out a hand to steady her. "I will sleep in your bed again," Karn said sourly to Tsusiat, who sighed and nodded, leaning back against Jenia. The old woman shuffled off into Tsusiat's alcove and blew out the lamp there.

The ginger warmth of Tsusiat's shoulders was starting to make Jenia feel drowsy with comfort. She had never thought to feel so peaceable, to feel anything at all again after the wizard had turned on her. A man came quietly among the benches and the visitors sitting on the wooden floor. When he met her gaze for a moment, Jenia saw it was the slave leather worker, who waved a crooked finger at her before turning back to collect empty bowls. She remembered that gesture, that good-natured gibe meaning, "do not take yourself too seriously," and she took it to heart. So if she was a wizard after all, it seemed she was only a minor wizard. A very little hedge-witch, something like Karn. The knowledge did not upset her.

Not even the arrival of Ronay into the circle of firelight could upset her. He approached warily, careful not to intrude. Talas was close behind and guided him to a seat on the other side of the open hearth. "I have brought Ronay here," said Talas. "Now that he and Jenia have eaten and rested a little, and now that we have heard Karn tell of her vision, there are some things that should be said with both Jenia and Ronay together."

The meat and vegetables Jenia had been given sat in the bowl on the bench beside her. She was so tired she'd barely been able to eat a few bites before setting the bowl down. But she felt as secure and solid leaning against Tsusiat as she would bracing herself against one of the solid posts of this great house.

"We have a request to make of Captain Ronay," said Talas, surprising Jenia. She'd expected Ronay would want to be the first to speak. Pressing forward into the circle of firelight were a dozen or more of the Tlakwa people, and some of the people who had been working on the tower in the crooked wood. Others hovered, near enough to hear what was being said by the fire.

"We have many visitors now," said Talas. "These are people rescued from Krummholz by Jenia and Karn, with your help. These visitors are welcome to stay with us for many days, to recover their strength, before returning to their homes." Talas spoke as if to Ronay alone, but was clearly aware of those around him, listening and nodding.

"If they can return to their homes," Tsusiat pointed out. "I think some of them are from very far away indeed, much farther than Jenia walked from her valley home. Do you see the embroidery on that woman's night-dress? I have never seen or heard tell of anything like it, not the patterns nor the stitches. Lady, Lema who makes our clothing will want to talk with you," Tsusiat said to the stranger-woman, who hid her face in soft, blistered hands, not understanding.

"Some may choose to stay with us, or to live in Opitsat, which is a larger village in the winter." Talas rocked forward on his wooden stool, elbows on knees, looking intently at Ronay. "When you leave our island, will you and your soldiers escort some of these people to the mainland?"

"Yes, I will be their escort," said Ronay. "For those who want to leave. I will even travel round the shoreline, rather than overland across the high ground that your people call forbidden," he added.

"That would be wise," Talas said with an air of formal approval. "Though Tsusiat has told me Jenia says the land is no longer poisoned and dangerous, there may still be strange beasts living inland. The high ground will still be forbidden to us for some time. And even our few shoreline paths will not be safe for strangers. It is good of you to escort them safely to the traders' boats to the mainland."

He looked at his hands, callused by paddle and carving knife. "And for those who were the wizard's guards..." Talas hesitated. "You are a soldier, in service to a powerful man. What do think of those who are now your prisoners?"

"I will take their parole," Ronay announced. "I will take them with me to Kultis, to join the service and swear allegiance to Lord Regis."

That particular idea had clearly not occurred to Talas. He rocked back on his stool. "That would take this problem out of our hands," he admitted. "We have never before had prisoners with no family or leader to ransom them. Nor do we need new slaves with such vicious habits."

"What will you do if any of them do not wish to serve your lord?" asked Tsusiat, without turning.

"My soldiers and I will take the prisoners up onto the headland, to the questioning place, and offer them the opportunity to enlist," Ronay said. "We will come down with the new recruits." There was no need for him to say more.

Jenia couldn't think of anything to say in favour of or against Ronay's plan. *There doesn't seem to be any other choice,* she knew. She groped for her bowl and ate more of the unfamiliar roots. It had been a long time since she had eaten the foods of home, she realized. *If I'm starting to miss eating turnips, it'll soon be time to start heading home.*

"Jenia? Ronay has a question for you." Talas waited for the murmuring voices outside the hearth to become quiet again, then looked expectantly at the captain.

"Will you return with me to Kultis, as my wife?"

That wasn't the question she had been expecting. Her jaw dropped, and she gaped like a fish. "As your...." It felt like Tsusiat's blanket had unravelled and come apart into threads piling up around her ankles, leaving her bare as any of the little children staring from their family's alcoves. Never had she understood that Ronay might ask this of her. Now she realized she had been unwilling to understand; as she had not been seeking a husband, she had not imagined anyone could seek a wife in her, and so had never listened too closely to what he had to say.

Stiffly, he took something from a pouch tied to his belt, and held it out for her. Numbly, she took it in her hand and looked to see what he had given her. It was the bird she had carved. He had rubbed the smooth wood with oil or grease to finish it. She still couldn't tell if the bird were asleep or dead. Wordlessly, she shook her head and gave it back to him, and he put it away in his pouch.

His mouth set, crooked as the slant in his nose. Then he asked the question she had been expecting from him, for which she had already prepared an answer. "Will you return with me to Kultis, and take service there as the Tree-Tender?"

"No. I will not travel with you." Jenia waited to be sure he believed her, and would not ask again. Then, slowly, words came to her as she gazed into the fire. "I will rest here for the summer. I will carve a walking staff from my twisted branch, and a whistle from a bone of Karn's whale. I will make sand villages with Lop, and tell stories, and gather food with Tsusiat. When it is almost time for the equinox storms to come to Copper Island, I will go to Kultis as a visitor, and I will do autumn pruning in the great orchard there. And then I will go home. I've had enough of wizards and war. My work here is done. I miss my apple trees."

She looked up from the cedar log coals. She had managed to surprise Ronay. "I will rely on you to send word to the traders at Musky Creek, to tell me whether your lord will allow me to leave Kultis. If he promises not to trap me, I will come there. If the autumn pruning goes well, I will ask my people if any of them wish to work in Kultis."

There was a silence while Ronay seemed to take in what she had said. Eventually he cleared his throat. "We will respect that," he said shortly. "I will send word to the traders at Musky Creek, to tell you my lord's wishes for you and his orchard."

Though she now trusted Ronay to keep his word, Jenia was not sure he could convince his lord not to keep her as a prisoner. Privately, she resolved to take passage far to the south in the traders' boats if Ronay's message did not give her confidence. There was no reason she had to return home the way she had already travelled, after all.

"It will be good to have you stay here for the summer," Talas said. He seemed relieved at this turn of events. "Perhaps you will continue to stay in Karn's house, and learn what she can teach you about the affairs of wizards."

"Karn can certainly teach me about herbs, at least. There are several she grows that I've never —"

"Karn is dead."

The hissing of the coals in the open hearth was the only sound under the roof of the great house. Talas took an armful of wood from the leather worker standing silently beside him, and threw it into the fire. After a long moment, the pine wood flared up in bright flames that broadened the circle of light around the hearth. "What are you saying?"

Tsusiat's voice never needed to be raised to carry to every corner. "Karn lay down to sleep in my bed. She will not wake again."

"How can you know that?" Talas whispered, while Lema darted into Tsusiat's dark alcove. Jenia began to wonder if the magic Karn had sensed was not from herself, but Tsusiat.

"You know me, brother." Tsusiat was bonelessly limp against Jenia's shoulder. "I sing the funeral chants, too."

Jenia put her arm around those broad shoulders and slim, corded arms, to hold Tsusiat from falling. But Tsusiat's dark head was bowed, not from fainting but in prayer; and that penetrating voice filled every alcove, chanting in subtle rhythm. Other voices joined in, and as the murmur of quiet speech rose again it never drowned out the chant that went on, as easy as drawing breath.

More fish were set to roast, and bowls were filled again for those who still hungered; some visitors lay down to rest limbs strained by unfamiliar labour, while others rocked and wept, confused and far from home. Ronay and his soldiers took their prisoners out onto the headland to the questioning place, while Talas walked the curve of the home beach, to check that every boat was pulled high enough on shore that the high tide, turning now, would not draw the boats away with the waves as it ebbed.

Over the village, with the smoke that rose from smoke holes in the roofs of the four great houses and with the light that spilled from their open doors, spread the chant that continued till Jenia knew the words as well as the tune, till she was singing too. The chant blended with conversation and stories, and with the quiet sounds of children sleeping, neither dominating nor drowned out. Sometimes in many voices, sometimes in few, sometimes only one that never faltered even during the burial, that chant filled Jenia; and her heart was healed by it.

Her memories ever after that summer tied that chant and the smoke of red cedar and white pine together with the grit of sand villages and with mouths stained purple from berries harvested from canes without thorns. She carved a bone whistle that sounded like Lop's squeal, and Lema made for her another bag to carry, for gifts of dried food for travel and beads to decorate clothing for her and for Dela, in hopes they would celebrate together, a new husband or a new babe. The funeral chants that had seemed so empty at Tared's funeral were now filled in her heart, so that when at last she came to lay the branch of twisted wood on his grave, it seemed Tsusiat's unfaltering voice sustained her and sang with her every step of the long way home.

Don't miss out!

Visit the website below and you can sign up to receive emails whenever Paula Johanson publishes a new book. There's no charge and no obligation.

https://books2read.com/r/B-A-ZKUK-GUOIB

BOOKS 2 READ

Connecting independent readers to independent writers.

Did you love *Tower in the Crooked Wood*? Then you should read *Plum Tree*[1] by Paula Johanson!

[2]

Driving with her Dad to visit Aunt May is his idea of how to help Tina out of a depression that's lasted months. But the highway is boring, the weather is hot, and she's seen enough rocks and sticks for a lifetime. Tina is so preoccupied with her thoughts and memories that she hardly sees the world changing around her. When Tina and her Dad stop in a small town that hasn't changed much since 1918, it's a chance for her thoughts and memories to shuffle into an order that might make a little more sense.

New from Doublejoy Books is the short novel *Plum Tree*, a story of transition from place to place and time to time. There's no fanfare or surprise when Tina meets young Tim, who lost his mother to the Spanish flu. As she shifts from childhood to youth, from present to past and future, she's thinking of how to connect her music with people. As Tina says, *Local stories. There could*

---

1. https://books2read.com/u/boEZ10

2. https://books2read.com/u/boEZ10

be a lot of them, especially if you didn't need them to be about guns and crimes but maybe about sports or inventing things. Or just ordinary life but as if it counted.

Read more at books2read.com/paulaj.

Also by Paula Johanson

Prime Ministers of Canada
Pierre Elliott Trudeau: Child of Nature
Charles Tupper: Warhorse

Slice of Life
No Parent Is An Island

Young Science
Bat Poop Sparkles

Standalone
Small Rain and Other Nightmares
Island Views
Plum Tree
Tower in the Crooked Wood
King Kwong: Larry Kwong, the China Clipper Who Broke the NHL Colour
Barrier
Woolgathering: Awareness of the Foreign in Published Works About
Cowichan Woolworking
Science Critters
Green Paddler

Watch for more at books2read.com/paulaj.

About the Author

Paula Johanson is a Canadian writer. A graduate of the University of Victoria with an MA in Canadian literature, she has worked as a security guard, a short order cook, a teacher, newspaper writer, and more. As well as editing books and teaching materials, she has run an organic-method small farm with her spouse, raised gifted twins, and cleaned university dormitories. In addition to novels and stories, she is the author of forty-two books written for educational publishers, among them *The Paleolithic Revolution* and *Women Writers* from the series *Defying Convention: Women Who Changed The World*. Johanson is an active member of SF Canada, the national association of science fiction and fantasy authors.

Read more at books2read.com/paulaj.

DOUBLEJOY BOOKS

About the Publisher

Doublejoy Books is the publisher of a variety of eclectic books of Canadian literature.

http://doublejoybooks.com
http://books2read.com/paulaj